Never Again

Angela Sanders

Never Again © 2018 Angela Sanders

Cover designed by Christian Bentulan, Covers by Christian

ISBN-13: 978-1724863652

ISBN-10: 1724863657

Acknowledgements and Dedications

This book is dedicated to anyone who has ever been a victim of abuse in any form—and lived. You are not a victim; you are a survivor.

Never Again is very personal to me, and although it is fiction, you will find pieces of my soul scattered throughout.

Never Again

She fought to leave her past behind her, but for Charlotte, there is no escape.

New Orleans Homicide Detective, Charlotte Pierce, was on the hunt for a sadistic serial killer who was known for slicing his prey, when she nearly became his ninth victim.

In an effort to leave her past behind her, she walked away from her profession to start a new life, until a copycat killer hit too close to home.

Now Charlotte must work with the department to find the killer and put this nightmare to rest once and for all, but that means facing her demons, and reliving the trauma she's tried so hard to forget.

When people close to her start dying, she knows she's going to be next. Charlotte refuses to be another victim. She won't let it happen.

Never again.

Chapter 1

I felt the cold slice of a knife as it slid down my left cheek, yet I refused to cry out. I wasn't going to allow that sick bastard the pleasure of seeing a hint of emotion pass across my face. Chained to a dank basement wall—the only light shone from a small bulb dangling from the middle of the ceiling—I could almost make out the evil glint in his eyes as he took pleasure in torturing me.

"My dearest Charlotte, your detective colleagues will never find you here. You're all alone." My captor's beady brown eyes roamed over my body, and then he ripped my blouse open, exposing my flesh.

I remained silent, determined not to give in to his taunts. Little did he know, I'd called for backup before I entered the premises. Francis Medley—wanted serial killer—and I just happened to be first on the scene once we learned of his location. It was by chance that I was off duty and had heard it called over the radio. My thoughts had raced immediately, thinking this would be it—we were finally taking the sadistic monster down for good. In my haste, and error in judgment, I went it alone without waiting for my partner.

Francis had left a calling card on all eight female victims: a diamond-shaped strip of flesh, expertly cut from their abdomen—death by asphyxiation—but not without torture. Their bodies were left with multiple lacerations—some with their tongues removed—but always, the same calling card. He'd escaped us for nine months, but we'd finally gotten a break on his latest victim, Tracy Harlan. He had been sloppy and left a small trace of DNA.

At twenty-seven, I'd been working for the New Orleans Homicide Unit for only a year, finally working my way up and earning my detective badge. It was something I had always wanted to do since witnessing my parents' brutal murder at the age of seven. I was bounced around from foster home to foster home, until at the age of ten, a wonderful family, Dan and Leanne Pierce, had adopted me. From then on, they made sure I had the best of everything, making up for the childhood that had been stolen from me.

Francis had taken me down with a blow to the head, removing my service weapon, just after I'd deemed the front room secure. He had been hiding in a makeshift secret passageway that I hadn't noticed—*rookie mistake*. Now, I was hanging by chains, experiencing a taste of what his earlier victims had before he'd murdered them.

My heart beat frantically in my chest. To say I was scared to death would have been an understatement. When I'd been investigating the murders, I'd always tried to put myself in the victims' shoes in order to get into the mind of the serial killer—feel what he was feeling: the motive, the connection. Now, I was experiencing it firsthand.

The blade slid down my stomach, making a deep cut, and I couldn't help but wince. "Scream, little bird. No one can hear you." His eyes lit up with something that looked like desire, and it sickened me to the core.

This bastard needed to die a long and painful death. Screw the justice system. If I were to break free, I was going to kill him myself, so he could never hurt another living soul. I'd ask for forgiveness later. And where the hell was my backup?

Francis grabbed my hair, yanking my head back so I would look at him. My blue eyes were cold as ice. He held the steel blade close to my cheek. Just as he was about to slice the corner of my mouth, I spat in his face.

Slamming my head against the concrete wall, he released his grip from my coal-black hair. "You'll pay dearly for that, bitch."

I glared back defiantly, still not saying a word. *Let him come near me again.* I had a will of steel—one he could *not* break.

Rushing toward me with his blade raised high, Francis was clearly aiming to bring it down on my head, but I jerked away just in time, then brought up my knee, crushing his balls. *Take that, fucker.*

He fell to the concrete floor, and I heard the clang of the knife. Panicking, I searched for it in the dimly lit basement, but the only thing I could see was a toolbelt with metal flaying instruments, lying across a long wooden table situated in the middle of the room. I gulped down my fear and said a quick prayer that maybe, just maybe, he wouldn't get up. How had I not noticed that godforsaken torture table before?

Francis was moaning when he lifted himself from the floor. "Want to play it rough, do you? Let's play a game." He limped over to the torture table from hell, and I felt my heart nearly gallop out of my chest. If my backup didn't arrive soon, I would surely be his next victim. How damn long did it take? It was midnight for God's sake!

I watched as he stroked his knives one-by-one, like they were some kind of precious toys, and felt the urge to vomit. Hot tears were threatening to spill, but I held them back. There was no way in hell I was going to allow that piece of shit to see me cry.

With a sneer, Francis turned around holding a serrated blade in his right hand. "This will work perfectly." He strode toward me in what seemed like slow motion. My mouth became dry, knowing what was to come. I wasn't sure if I could maintain my silence any longer once that knife carved into my skin.

I yanked and pulled on my chains, but I was secured tightly to the wall with very little slack. The only part of my body that I could move freely was my torso and legs. If I was going to die, I was going down with one hell of fight. I bucked wildly the closer he came, and the only sound I could hear was the clanging of the chains that held me, and his maniacal laughter.

"Come any closer, and I promise you, I *will* kill you," I growled, lunging forward, my tone deep and deadly.

"Music to my ears." He continued to advance slowly as if stalking his prey. "Keep singing, little bird."

I shut my mouth, knowing he was getting his rocks off. I decided to wait until he was close enough to make my next move.

Without warning, I felt searing pain in my right leg—the son of a bitch had thrown the knife and hit his target. I held back my cry, throwing my head against the wall. Sweat was dripping down my face. I knew I was losing a lot of blood; my vision became blurred, and dizziness washed over me. Then I felt a *whoosh* as the knife was ripped from my body, and I sank to the floor with only chains holding me upright.

Another strike, this time in my left arm. Darkness ebbed my vision, and the last thing I saw was the face of evil, masked behind beady brown eyes and long, greasy brown hair, then nothingness.

Six Weeks Earlier

"Hey, Mamma." I kissed her on the cheek, taking a seat at the oak wood kitchen table situated in front of a bay window overlooking the spacious backyard.

Today was Sunday, and we were supposed to be having our regularly scheduled breakfast, but Mom seemed off, and there was no food on the table. Her blue eyes were red rimmed, and her normally perfectly coifed blonde hair was somewhat disheveled.

Tears slid down her face, streaking what looked like last night's makeup. "Charlotte, I have something I want to speak with you about." She took a deep breath and sighed. "You know the young girl your team found the other night, Ginger Walters?"

I nodded but didn't interrupt. I wondered where my dad was. Mom was a wreck. She was always so calm and collected; I'd never seen her in such a state.

"Before your father and I adopted you, we used to babysit Ginger. I've known her since she was born." Mom swiped an errant tear from her face, then looked down at her hands. "I'd lost touch with her and her mother over the years, but when I saw the news reports, I knew it was Ginger right away. Her face hasn't changed." She reached over and clasped my hand. "I'm scared for you, honey. This killer is murdering innocent young women your age."

"Mamma, I'm sorry about Ginger. I know you're worried"—I squeezed her hand tight—"but we have the best detectives in New Orleans on the case. We're getting close. I can feel it."

Mom stood from her seat to pour us each a cup of coffee. She handed me a cup and then sat back down with a worried expression. "Your father isn't taking any chances. He's looking into an alarm system as we speak. I really think it's best if you stay with us for a while—"

"Mom," I cut her off. "I'm twenty-seven years old, and I'm working this case. I've done nothing but eat, sleep, and breathe it. I'm not sure why you're so worried; you know I can protect myself."

"I know." She looked past me and glanced out of the window into the backyard. "Do you remember much about your life before you came to us?"

I swallowed hard. Yes, I did, but I didn't like to discuss it. "Yeah, a little." I took a sip of my coffee as horrific memories of my birthparents' murder flashed before my eyes.

Faint sounds of gunshots rang in my ears, and I closed my eyes to wash away the ghosts of my past.

"You were so young and had seen so much for a child your age. I made a promise to myself then that I would always protect you and keep you from harm's way." She turned to look at me with a small smile. "I'm proud of the woman you've become, Charlotte, although I worry for you each and every day. The life of a homicide detective... You have no idea what that feels like."

"Mom," I attempted to interrupt her.

She held up her hand. "No, let me finish."

"Okay."

"It's a mother's instinct to protect her child. That never goes away; it doesn't matter if you're ten or fifty. I never wanted this kind of life for you, but after what you lived through, I always knew this would be your path.

"Then to learn about Ginger's death. She lived in this neighborhood, did you know that?" She wiped the tears from her face, but they continued to fall.

"Yes, Mamma." I wasn't sure where she was going with this, but I knew I had to let her finish. She was distraught.

"She could have been you, Charlotte. That's all I can think about. She could have been you." Mom lost what was left of her composure and broke down into heaving sobs.

I couldn't take anymore and stood to hug her. She was breaking my heart. Something was telling me there was more to the story, but I didn't have the heart to ask. She would tell me when she was ready.

"I'm okay, Mamma. I'm right here, and I'm not going anywhere. Look at me." I tilted her tear-streaked face, so we were eye level. "I'm trained for homicide. I promise you, we will do everything we can to find this sick piece of crap."

"That's what I'm afraid of, Char. I don't want you doing this anymore. Your father and I are so worried, we can't even sleep," she said through a sob. "We thought maybe it was a coincidence, but now, we're not so sure."

My hackles rose. "What are you talking about? What coincidence?"

Mom straightened in her chair and stared at me pointedly. "I didn't want to say anything, but after Ginger, it's all just too much. We've been receiving threatening phone calls by unknown numbers, and just two days ago, the neighbor's cat was left on our back porch with its throat slit." Her hands began to tremble slightly.

My eyes bulged, and my heart nearly stopped. "What? Why haven't you called the police? Why didn't you tell me? Mom, this is serious shit!" I couldn't believe she would keep this to herself. What the hell kind of sicko does something like that? Kills a cat? The fu—

"Charlotte, must you use that kind of language? For heaven's sake." She eyed me with the "Mom look." "We just thought it was a bunch of kids fooling around. We talked with a few of our neighbors, and they'd been getting the same harassing phone calls. We didn't think it was a big deal. But then the cat and Ginger..." She trailed off, shaking her head.

"This isn't something you just overlook, Mom. It could be serious. I'm going to have someone take a look at your call records. Did you happen to write down the time of these phone calls, or remember what was said?"

"It's been happening over the past several weeks. I can't be sure, but the calls always came in around eight p.m., and always from an unknown number. The caller's voice was tampered with or something." She waved her hand around her head in dismissal. "It sounded automated. He would say things like, 'watch your back old lady,' or ask obscene questions. I just hung up on him. He was vile."

"Did Dad ever answer the phone?" I was livid. I would find out who was threatening my parents. I also wondered if this had anything to do with Ginger as Mom suspected. It wasn't very likely, but something to look into, at least the threatening phone calls.

"No, you know how he is. He never answers the phone." She rolled her eyes. "Would you like some more coffee?"

Good grief. We were talking about harassing phone calls and a dead cat on her doorstep, and she was asking about coffee. I now understood why she was so worried about me, but why wasn't she more worried about herself? None of this made any sense.

"Sure. Thanks, Mamma."

She set a fresh cup of black coffee in front of me, and I took a sip. "How much longer until Dad gets home?"

"Who knows with him? He'll probably stake out every security system in Jefferson Parish." She smiled knowingly. "Sorry about breakfast. I've just been a mess, and I needed to talk to you about all of this. I feel better now that you know. Promise me you'll be careful, Charlotte."

"I will, Mamma. But you need to be careful, too. I'm gonna see if we can find a link in those phone calls. Not sure about the cat, but I'd venture to guess it might be the same person or *persons*. If it's a bunch of kids, they're probably serial killers in the making." I visibly shuddered at the thought.

"All right, Char. Thank you. I love you, honey." She leaned over and kissed my cheek. "Just be careful. Let me know if there's anything I can do to help."

"Will do, Mamma. I need to run. Tell Dad I love him, and I'll see him later." I stood from the table and put my coffee mug in the sink.

She walked me to the door and hugged me goodbye. I waved one last time from my black unmarked police cruiser, and then took the drive toward the station.

When I walked through the bullpen, it was crazy as usual. Phones were ringing, the smell of burnt coffee wafted through the air, and florescent lights flickered, casting shadows along the old wood-paneled walls. I walked to my desk and tossed my coat over the back of my chair, then fired up my computer.

Today was my day off, but after what Mom had told me, I decided to pull her phone records. I thought just maybe I might get lucky and find something out of the ordinary.

I'd asked Mom to call me once my dad had the new security system installed; I wanted complete access to it just in case.

Sergeant Jeff Belafonte rested his hip on the corner of my desk. "What are you doing here? I thought you were off today."

I didn't look up from my computer. "I am."

"Okay. Anything I can help you with?"

I could feel his eyes boring a hole into my head, so I looked up into his chestnut-colored eyes. "As a matter of fact, yes. I went to visit my mom today. And it could be nothing, but I'd like for you to look into these phone records for me. She and her neighbors have been receiving threatening calls, ones she neglected to tell me or the police about." I handed him the list I'd just printed with incoming phone calls made in the past month. "All phone calls take place around eight p.m. from an unknown number. Is there any way you can work with our data team and see if anything can be drawn from this list?" He nodded and took the list. "Mom also mentioned something about a possible connection to Ginger Walters; she used to babysit her before I came along."

Sergeant Belafonte eyed me curiously. "What do you think? Is there a connection?"

Damn, if I had time to date, and if he weren't a coworker, Jeff would definitely be my type.

Standing at six feet four inches tall, Jeff Belafonte had dark brown hair, light brown skin, square jaw, and sky-blue eyes with just a touch of green, resting above a symmetrical nose and full kissable lips. His hard body couldn't be missed by the way it filled out his crisp uniform. This was why I tried not to look at him. I needed to keep my mind on the job, and it was *not* easy when he talked to me in his slow Southern drawl.

Mind out of gutter. Now.

I cleared my throat and the cobwebs from my head. "I don't know, but we can never be too sure. My mom was really upset, and this just pushes me over the edge. We have to find that son of a bitch before he murders his next victim." I squeezed my fists together under my desk, thinking about what had happened, feeling my blood boil. My earlier thoughts of Jeff went out the window. "Ginger lived in my parents' neighborhood; this much we know. My mom is devastated, and now it's personal. I'm not sleeping until we find this prick."

"Understood. I'll see what I can do on my end. Look over the case files again and go to the white board. I'll meet you there in a few. Maybe we're missing something."

I grabbed the case files from my desk and went to the break room to pour myself a cup of coffee that looked like mud, and probably tasted like burnt coffee grounds. I took a sip— it did—but caffeine was caffeine and burnt mud would have to do for now.

I stood before the white board, looking at the photos of all seven victims, and my stomach dropped when I saw the wreck that was left of Ginger Walters. My mother knew her. In my mind, I knew I had to separate myself and look at each victim with a technical eye: What had I missed? Was there anything that could lead us to the identity of the killer? Instead, I continued to look at Ginger and think about my mom and dad. Who was harassing them? Was any of this connected? I knew I needed to get a grip, or I wouldn't be able to do my job.

Shaking my hands out to the side and taking a deep breath, I closed my eyes, then began to focus on what I did know.

Like pieces of a puzzle forming in my mind, I glanced at the faces of all the women, and their lifeless bodies; how they were killed and put on display, then cut with precision. Two victims had their tongues cut out and placed near their left ear, both, exactly the same.

Why were these two different from the others? The diamond-shaped wound on their abdomens held the same calling card as the other victims. These women must have done something the killer deemed untrustworthy; he'd made it personal. I closed my eyes, concentrating on the similarities and anything that might be hidden from the human eye, a code of sorts.

The deep lacerations were still on the left side of their faces. Their tongues had been strategically placed near their left ear.

What does the left side signify?

The common word, left, comes from the Latin word, sinister...

Were the lacerations on the left side of their faces a missing piece of the puzzle we'd yet to put together?

Sinister... Foreboding... An impression that something harmful or evil would happen or be spoken.

Speak, hear... Tongue, ear... Connection... Did he know the victims?

Something was beginning to click when Jeff walked into the situation room, startling me from my thoughts. "Dammit! You scared the shit out of me."

"Sorry, Detective." He smiled a crooked smile, enjoying my flushed face. He seriously needed to stop.

"Did you find anything?" I smoothed my sweaty hands over my black slacks and grabbed my cup of now-cold coffee.

"Not yet, but we have time. It looks like the calls were made from a burner phone. Not surprising."

I huffed in frustration. "Who the hell would do something like that? I mean, prank calls and a dead cat? It's freakin' sadistic and creepy. My main concern is, what if the same thing was happening to Ginger, since she lived in the same neighborhood?" I set my mug on the table. "Do we have her phone records yet?"

"Yep. Cindy just got them." He placed the files on the table and took a seat. "I thought we could look them over together, if you don't mind."

Of course I minded. *Damn.* "No, it's fine. Maybe we'll find a link, if not, at least I know my dad's getting a security system."

We pored over page after page of freakin' phone records until we found it—the link. Dammit! Mom was right. An unknown number had been calling Ginger for weeks, almost immediately after calling my parents. I didn't believe in coincidences. Now, I just had to find out who that damn burner phone belonged to.

I went home for the night, still mulling over the connection between the severed tongues and the word "sinister." Something in my gut told me this was the missing piece we'd been looking for; the killer had deviated, and it was quite possible he knew those two victims.

What had the women said that caused him to remove their tongues? Was it biblical in reference, or just a sick twisted game he was playing to throw us off track? The right side was typically in reference to the "right hand of God." Yet the killer had chosen the left. Was it possible he was acting out his vengeance toward God in an attempt to play God himself? Did something happen in his past to make him feel slighted by God?

Maybe we were looking at this from the wrong angle. We could be looking for someone who thought the church, or God had forsaken him.

The diamond-shaped pattern came to mind. What was its significance? Immortality, or the semblance of nature, encouraging the aspect of truth and trust... Was that it? Were the calling cards his own wacked out brand of immortality, seeking out truth, reveling in his victims' death?

Untrustworthy... The tongues being removed. There was a link between the two; I just had to put them together.

***

Another freakin' body. My partner called me at two a.m., and I lost my shit. I thought for sure we were on our way to locating the serial killer, but no. He'd struck again, and this time, right under our noses. I was pissed. I'd done nothing but work my ass off and had barely slept, trying to piece everything together. I thought for sure I'd found the connection, working tirelessly to link the killer to all seven victims. I was closing in fast—I had leads—or so I'd thought. Now this? Another murder, and I felt responsible.

Pulling into Audubon Park, my stomach clenched. I walked slowly toward the line of uniformed officers and slid under the crime scene tape after presenting my badge. My partner, Greg, was already there waiting for me with the ME. The woman's body had been staged on a park bench near the waterfront under a large oak tree.

"Hey, Char," Greg greeted me, then proceeded to give me the run-down.

I watched as the ME carefully looked over each laceration, while the forensic team took pictures of anything they deemed evidentiary. All I could see was *her*—the exact same calling card—everything I'd been working hard to prevent from happening again. My heart thudded in my chest, and I felt like I was about to explode. What could I have done to stop this? It was as if the killer knew we were onto him, and this was all some sort of game. This woman's death was my fault. I couldn't breathe.

Chapter 2
Present Day

The strong smell of antiseptic assaulted my senses when I felt myself coming back to the world of the living. The *beep, beep, beep* of machines sounding off let me know I was in the hospital. But how did I get here? I thought for sure I was dead.

My eyelids were heavy, and my body hurt all over—it felt like I'd been hit by a truck and then rolled into oncoming traffic again. The sound of someone's heavy breathing alerted me that I wasn't alone. I attempted to open my eyes, but they felt like I'd been caught in a sandstorm with no eye protection. I slowly cracked my eyes open to find my partner, Greg Stevenson, asleep in the chair next to my bed.

Clearing my throat, I tried to speak. "Hey." It sounded like gravel. I needed water in a bad way.

Greg jumped from his chair. "You're awake! Damn, you gave us a scare. How ya feelin'?"

I just looked at him like a dumb ass. "Water."

"Oh, yeah. Sorry." He grabbed a pitcher of water from the table next to my bed, and poured me a cup with a straw, then held it so I could take a sip.

"When we found you, I..." He paused, taking a deep breath. "I'm sorry, Char. That son of a bitch is behind bars now."

I turned my head to face him. He looked like shit, with messy dishwater-brown hair and red rimmed whiskey-colored eyes. He must have slept in his clothes.

"Good. I hope he dies there."

"Captain came by earlier. He wants to ask you some questions." Greg shifted in his seat, looking uncomfortable.

"Yeah? Hand me that water, would ya? And help me sit up, if you don't mind?"

"Sure." He gently moved me to a sitting position, and it felt like the fires of hell were burning my insides. Maybe that wasn't such a good idea after all. I still didn't know the extent of my injuries. "Here's your water."

I winced in pain when I reached for the cup, and saw my hands were partially wrapped in gauze. Then I looked at my arms. I didn't want to see any more, so I braced for the pain, and took a generous gulp of water to clear the desert sand out of my mouth, then handed Greg the cup.

"Thanks, Greg."

"Char, I know this isn't easy, but as your partner, I need to know—are you gonna be all right?" His eyes were full of concern and what looked like regret.

"I'm not sure. I don't remember much after I passed out, but I'm sure it'll come back to me. How long have I been out?" My throat still felt scratchy.

"Four days."

I slumped back onto the bed and looked toward the ceiling, attempting to hold back the tears. Fleeting memories of what had happened that night plagued my mind, but I couldn't let that psychotic fucker beat me. He had no power over me. "Go ahead and call the captain now. I might as well get this over with."

Greg looked at me with pity in his eyes. What the hell? I really needed to know everything that had happened to me.

"All right. I'll just step out and make the call."

"No, just call him. What's the big secret?" I felt something was off, something he wasn't telling me.

"Char, you need to wait for the doctors, okay? I can't..." He hung his head, rubbing his hand nervously along the leg of his pants. "Just wait."

"What the hell are you not telling me, Greg? This is bullshit!" I cried out when it felt like stitches ruptured somewhere in my gut. I looked down and saw blood appear on my thin white blanket. *Just fucking great.* I pressed the call button for the nurse. "We're not done here." My breathing was ragged as the pain became unbearable.

Greg stood from the chair, looked at me with sad eyes, and stepped into the hallway.

A nurse, looking like Nurse Ratchet, came in just as he walked out. "Oh, my. You're bleeding."

No shit, Captain Obvious. "Yes. It just started."

"Let me take a look at it." Nurse Ratchet pulled the blanket back and then lifted my standard issue hospital gown. I had staples in my stomach. Staples! "It looks like we're going to have to get this taken care of right away. I'm calling the doctor now."

I just laid my head back while she tried to control the bleeding until the doctor arrived.

She put something in my IV, and off to dreamland I went.

Chapter 3

I awoke to the steady beep of my heart monitor, and the sickening smell of antiseptic again, reminding me that I was still alive and in the hospital. I wondered if anyone had called my mom and dad. I'd been in here for four days, but the only person I'd seen so far was Greg.

I pressed the call button for my nurse and waited. This time it wasn't Nurse Ratchet, it was another nurse: a petite blonde with tanned skin. She introduced herself as Emily.

"Hello, Charlotte. Good to see you awake. How are you feeling?"

"As good as I can be, I guess." I shifted a little to get comfortable. I hated hospital pillows. They were so damn sticky. "Has anyone called my parents, or have they stopped by? Dan and Leanne Pierce?"

Emily's face went pale. "You don't know?"

"Know what?"

"Maybe it'll be better if I call Captain Davis to come back in and talk to you. He's been waiting for several hours."

"What the hell is going on, and why won't anyone tell me anything?"

Emily took a step back. "I'm sorry, Charlotte, but I believe it's best if you speak with your captain. I'll get him now." Then she rushed out of the door.

My heart began thundering in my chest. I had no idea why everyone was being so fucking secretive around me, like I was some kind of child. I was attacked by a serial killer and lived. I was a damned detective. Shit happened. People needed to start talking, or I was gonna lose my shit in that hospital.

Captain Marshall Davis walked in interrupting my internal rant. His normal crisp appearance was disheveled, and he had dark circles beneath his hazel eyes. It seemed like his salt-and-pepper hair had grayed even more since the last time I'd seen him.

"Captain."

"Detective." He took a seat in the chair next to my bed.

"I'm just gonna forget the formalities here, considering I'm lying in this bed, and no one will answer my questions. Why did that nurse just run outta here like her ass was on fire at the mention of my parents?"

Captain Davis scrubbed his hand over his face and then looked down at his shoes. After a moment, he glanced back up. "Charlotte, there's no easy way to say this, so I'll just be straight with you. Francis Medley killed your parents the day"—he paused, and I choked— "the day you were attacked. We found pictures of you and your family in his greenroom. He'd been stalking you."

I couldn't hold back the tears. My parents; the only people left in this world who truly gave a damn about me—gone—murdered—by the same man who'd tortured, and nearly killed me. How did I *not* know I was being stalked?

"Why?" I choked on a sob. "Why would he stalk me? My parents? They had a security system. Dad... I don't understand."

Captain Davis stood from the chair and walked toward the window. "It seems you were too close to the case. Remember Ginger Walters, the seventh victim?"

"Yeah." I began to feel the walls closing in around me.

"She lived near you, and that's how he found you, learned you were a detective on the case. He had a shrine of sorts."

"But my parents?" I couldn't stop the tears from falling. I knew I was probably going to bust another staple or stitch, but I didn't give a damn. It was connected… just like Mom had thought all along. That fucker deserved to burn in hell. And I still couldn't remember all that he had done to me.

"I'm sorry, Charlotte." Captain Davis walked back to my bed and placed his hand on my shoulder. "We're all here for you, and counseling will be made available when you recover."

"How the hell long am I supposed to stay in here?" I couldn't help but shout. Who was going to bury my parents? What the hell was I going to do?

"I don't know, but you've sustained severe injuries, many I'm not sure you're aware of." Captain Davis couldn't look me in the eye; he just stared at the floor.

"When will I know? Can you please tell a damn doctor to come in here? I'm not some fucking invalid."

The tears continued to fall as I thought of a life without my mom and dad.

"I'm sorry, Charlotte. I'll have the nurse get the doctor on call. You have my number if you need anything."

He still couldn't look at me. "Bye, Captain."

He walked out of the door with a slight wave, his head hung low.

I screamed at the top of my lungs. My heart shattered into a million pieces—that murderous piece of shit killed my parents, and I had done nothing to stop it. Mom had called me that morning, wanting me to stop by for coffee, but I was too busy. Why was I too busy? I couldn't even remember! Now she and Dad were just gone! I could've been there to stop him, but I was... *busy*. I continued to wail until someone entered the room. Even then, I sobbed uncontrollably. My parents were dead. I couldn't even kill the son of a bitch; he was locked away.

"Miss Pierce, please calm down. My name is Doctor Leslie, and I'm here to help you." He walked closer to my bed, but I didn't care. "Miss Pierce, please."

"My parents were murdered by a serial killer, who I couldn't stop, and you want me to calm down?" I looked at him incredulously.

"Would you like me to give you something to help calm your nerves?" He tried to hand me a box of tissues, but I ignored him.

"No, I want answers, dammit." I took a deep breath, realizing that it wasn't his fault, and then attempted to dry my face with my blanket. *Gross, but whatever.* "I'm sorry. I just learned my parents were murdered by the same man who attacked me. And I need to know the extent of my injuries so that I may find a way to bury"—I choked back a sob—"bury them."

"I understand, Miss Pierce. Do you mind if I sit?"

"No, please. It's fine." I didn't care if he sat or stood.

Doctor Leslie's blonde hair was swept to the side of his forehead, and his green eyes were hidden behind a pair of black horn-rimmed glasses. He looked to be in his mid-forties, but he seemed to be genuinely concerned about my well-being based on the look on his face.

"I'm afraid you have lacerations covering thirty percent of your body, Miss Pierce. You were also sexually assaulted, but your fellow officers found you while"—he paused to clear his throat, covering his mouth with his fist—"while the man was still...in the act. He used a serrated blade to cut your thighs, but—"

"You can stop now, Doctor Leslie," I interrupted. "I don't need to hear anymore. Once my wounds heal, I'm sure I'll see them for myself."

"I'm truly sorry, Miss Pierce—for everything you've had to endure. And your parents." He reached out to touch my gauze-covered hand, and I almost retracted but decided to allow it. He was being kind. "We have grief counselors on staff, along with chaplains, and professional associates for victims of sexual assault if you would like me to contact one of them for you."

"Thank you, but that won't be necessary." I took a calming breath, attempting to keep my heart from catapulting out of my chest. "How soon before I'm discharged, Doctor?"

"As soon as tomorrow, if you're feeling up to it, but you'll need to be careful of your injuries." He stood from his chair and patted my shoulder. "I'd honestly feel better if you stayed at least two more days for observation, but it's your call."

"Tomorrow would be nice. Thank you." I wanted to get the hell out of there now, wounds be damned.

"All right. If you need anything at all, please don't hesitate to call." He handed me his business card, gave me a small smile, and walked out of the door.

Chapter 4

The following day, I asked the nurse to remove the bandages from my hands and arms. I was on strict orders to come back in two weeks, so they could remove the staples from my stomach and stitches from nearly everywhere—no lifting, no physical activity, blah, blah, blah. I just wanted to get the hell out of there, so I could bury my mom and dad—who I learned were still in the morgue.

Thankfully, the captain had done me a solid, allowing them to remain there once the autopsies were completed, until I could claim the bodies, and have them moved to the funeral home of my choice. Generally, the process would have been much longer, but because he knew the victims, he'd put a rush on everything—for me.

This was when it hit me again that I was all alone. I wasn't sure if I could handle burying my parents and dealing with the trauma of what I'd just been through. Sure, everyone kept saying there were grief counselors. My partner had come by to check on me, but what could he do? I no longer felt like I was part of the team; they had let me down. I'd let myself down. I needed a fresh start, somewhere that wasn't New Orleans Homicide.

Standing in the small bathroom, I began to assess my injuries. Doctor Leslie hadn't been exaggerating when he'd said I had lacerations covering thirty percent of my body; it looked more like fifty percent to me. My arms, stomach, thighs, and even my face had taken quite a beating. I felt like Frankenstein. I didn't even look like myself: my eyes were black and bloodshot, and my lips were cut, swollen, and bruised. I had at least eighteen stitches running down the left side of my cheek where Francis had decided to use my face as some kind of sick art project. I decided I didn't want to see anymore. My face would heal eventually.

Carefully pulling on a loose, short-sleeved black T-shirt and a large pair of borrowed, dark blue drawstring scrub pants, I began to feel a bit more human. I'd called my friend, Nicky Bastille, to pick me up from the hospital once I identified the bodies of my parents. *My parents.* My heart was breaking all over again thinking of what I was about to do. I wasn't sure how I would be able to hold myself together. I didn't care what had happened to me, but the thought of seeing their lifeless bodies nearly broke me.

I wasn't allowed to walk to the morgue; a nurse took me by wheelchair. I closed my eyes, praying this was some kind of nightmare. When the elevator dinged announcing our arrival on the basement floor, my heart sank in my chest. I wasn't sure if I could go through with this. It felt like I was being led to my death, and I couldn't breathe; the walls began closing in around me.

"Charlotte, are you okay?" The dark-haired nurse leaned down, grasping my shoulders. I was falling forward in my wheelchair.

I couldn't reply. My chest felt tight, and I couldn't breathe. The green-colored walls became a blur, and the only sound I could hear was the buzzing in my ears. Blackness obscured my vision—in and out like an old black-and-white television set—fuzzy, then black again. Soon, there was nothing but static, and the erratic pounding of my heart.

Muffled voices sounded far off in the distance, but I couldn't make anything out. I was lost in a sea of despair, my heart crushed, and I didn't want to wake up to find that my nightmare was real. That everything I thought I'd imagined had actually happened—they were dead. Francis had killed them. It was my fault. If only—

"Charlotte!" My eyes snapped open, and I drew in a ragged breath. Captain Davis was leaning over me while I lay on a gurney in the corridor of the basement.

"What the hell? Why am I on this gurney?"

"You had a panic attack and passed out. Are you all right? Do you need a doctor?" The captain looked sick, with worry lines etched across his face.

"No. I'm fine... I think. Do you mind helping me up? Where's the nurse?" I looked around the puke-green hallway while Captain Davis extended his arm so I could sit up. I slowly slid my legs over the side of the gurney and then attempted to step down.

"No. You don't need to be walking just yet." He stopped my feet from touching the floor. "The nurse will be right back with your wheelchair. Are you sure you should be going home today? You don't look so well."

I frowned, attempting to rein in my temper. He wasn't my father. No. *My father* was dead. "I'll be fine after I identify the bodies and get home. It's not every day someone has to see—" I stopped myself from elaborating. I just couldn't, even though part of me wanted to be a smart ass. Now was not the time. I needed to pull myself together. My emotions were all over the place, and I didn't know which way was up. My heart... It hurt. I was shattered.

"I'm sorry, Char. I know this must be hard on you. Do you want me to go in with you?" I'd never seen the captain look near tears until that moment. I almost broke again.

"Thank you, Captain. I appreciate it, but I'll be okay. You can wait outside if you want."

He nodded and then patted me on the shoulder.

The same dark-haired nurse approached with my wheelchair, asking if I was ready to proceed. Holding back my tears, I shook my head while she helped me get into the chair and wheeled me toward the stainless-steel door.

Closing my eyes and taking a weary breath, I steeled my nerves for what I was about to see. When we arrived inside the morgue, the medical examiner was waiting. He gave me his condolences, and I asked him to please continue. I didn't want to prolong this any longer than I had to.

Opening the first metal drawer, I saw the blonde hair of my mother peeking out from the beneath the stark-white sheet. Without seeing her face, I knew it was her right away. Although I had seen my share of dead bodies in my profession, this was one body I didn't want to see. Unfortunately, the sheet was pulled back before I could protest.

I gasped, covering my mouth with my hands. My mom. My beautiful mother's face had been deeply cut across her left cheek— same as mine—and her mouth was sliced nearly from ear to ear. There were so many lacerations, her face was almost unrecognizable. The sadistic fuck had cut his diamond-shaped pattern from her right cheek instead of her abdomen, like his other victims.

I swung my head to the side and threw up on the floor. The pain my poor mother must have endured. *I was busy. She died.* I threw up again, dry heaving, and the nurse held my arms just as I was about to faceplant onto the floor. They had their identification. My tears and vomit were enough.

My dad was in much the same shape, but he had been violated in an even more gruesome manner. I only glanced for a moment and then nodded my head. I had to get out of there. What had happened to them was something you'd see in horror films. Something only a monster would do. Francis had shifted away from his usual calling card when he'd killed them. I assumed it was a sick surprise just for me.

Francis Medley had a surprise coming. He just didn't know it yet.

Chapter 5

Nicky arrived just after four p.m. to pick me up. I couldn't get out of that hospital fast enough. As soon as the muggy New Orleans air hit my face, I felt free. Seeing her blue Honda Accord pulling up to the curb, I stood from my wheelchair on shaky legs.

"Hey, girl. I brought you some coffee. It's better than the crap you get in this place," Nicky said, opening my door, and helping me into the passenger seat. Her long blonde hair was pulled back into a messy bun. I could see the tribal tattoo that snaked just below the sleeve of her black T-shirt, and she was wearing black yoga pants that hid her tattoo-covered legs. I was shocked she wasn't wearing shorts; she must have just come from the gym.

"Thanks, Nicky. I appreciate you doing this for me. How's everything at The Styx?"

The Styx was a bar located two blocks from our apartment on St. Charles Boulevard. Nicky had been the manager there for five years. We'd become friends after I'd moved into the apartment upstairs from her two years ago.

"Same ole, same ole. Ya know." She glanced away from the road when we came to a stoplight and pinned her blue eyes on me. "Char, you've been through hell and back, and you're asking about my bar? Really? I wanna know how you're holdin' up. I mean, I'm here if you need me."

I let out a breath and then took a sip of coffee. "I know you are. I just don't wanna talk about it right now. I'm sorry."

She gently patted me on the arm. "I can understand that. Just know when you are, I'm your girl."

Nicky had never been the affectionate type; she was more likely to punch you in the throat than hug you. The pat on my arm meant a lot. She was like the sister I never had. We were both tough as nails on the outside, but when it came to our friends, we'd do anything for them.

I laid my head back on the headrest and prepared for the drive to my apartment. I could feel Nicky's eyes on me throughout the entire trip and knew she was worried. I would eventually have to tell her what had happened to me, but today was not that day. I just wanted to crawl into my own bed and sleep— wake up, and everything be okay.

When we pulled into the parking lot of our apartment complex, I took a deep breath and exhaled. I was home, safe, and that was what mattered the most.

Nicky switched off the engine, got out, grabbing my bag, and then came around to the passenger side door to help me. I tried getting out on my own, but the staples in my stomach gave me a big thwack in my gut, letting me know that definitely wasn't gonna happen. So, I looked up at a scowling Nicky, and allowed her to grab under my arms and gently slide me out of the Honda, then onto my feet. This sucked. I felt so helpless.

The stairs were another matter. Why did I have to live on the second floor? I took each step carefully, with Nicky holding onto one arm, while I braced myself on the railing with the other. I was cursing internally the entire time. Once I made it to the front of my door, I felt like I'd run a freakin' marathon.

I turned the key and opened the door. "Thanks, Nicky. Looks like I'll be ordering take-out for a while. Those stairs are the devil."

Nicky laughed, setting my hospital bag near the side table. "Yeah, you would if you were staying by yourself, but that's not happening. You have a new roommate. Didn't you know?"

I turned and glared. "What? That's not funny, Nicky. I don't do roommates." I was about to get pissed.

"It's me, dumb-dumb. I'm staying with you until you're feeling better." She rolled her eyes. "You can't very well take care of yourself with staples and shit, let alone feed yourself. So, just deal with it." She walked across the room, taking a seat on my brown leather couch.

"Why didn't you just say that?" I smiled, giving her a goofy look. "Thanks. Again."

"No problem. I'll cash in on my favors later." She winked at me. "Do you want to lie down for a while? I can unpack your stuff and get things ready for ya."

"Sure. That sounds like a plan. I'm over this day and want my own bed."

"Come on, darlin'. Let's go." She stood from the sofa and helped me walk down the hallway to my bedroom located on the right-hand side. The door to my en suite master bath was situated on the far-left wall, close enough to my bed where I wouldn't have to walk too far if needed. I hadn't thought about it before, but right then, I was thankful.

When she opened the door, I felt relieved seeing my queen-sized bed stacked with pillows, covered in a navy blue down comforter. If not for my injuries, I would have fallen onto it face first.

Nicky opened my bag from the hospital. "I'll just throw this stuff in the laundry."

"No. Throw that shit in the trash. I don't wanna look at it!" I had fire in my eyes and felt my heart begin to race.

"All right. It's just the clothes Greg brought over for you to change into. The department has what you were wearing..." She trailed off with what looked like pain in her eyes.

I knew what she was going to say, but it didn't matter. I didn't want any reminders of that murderous man, or my stay in the hospital. I wanted to put it all behind me and move on—never think about it again.

"As a matter of fact, take the clothes I'm wearing, too. I don't want them. Give them to Goodwill or something. I don't care, just get rid of them. Please."

I knew I was being crass, and I was trying to keep my tone calm and even, but everything I said sounded like an order rather than a request. Nicky was my friend, my only true friend really, and treating her this way made me feel like shit. I just couldn't help it. My mind was spinning, and I just wanted to sleep, make it all go away.

"Whatever you need, Char. Here, let me help you, hon." Nicky stepped forward to help remove my shirt. When I tried to step out of my scrubs, I cried out in pain. Deciding to sit on the bed, I let her pull them off of me. I realized drawstrings didn't make a damn bit of difference when your gut was nearly split in half. Everything freakin' hurt.

Once the offensive garments were out of my sight, I could finally breathe again. "I'm sorry for the way I talked to you, Nicky. You don't deserve that." I hung my head and allowed the tears to roll down my cheeks.

"Hey. Look at me." She placed her hands on my face. "You've been through something most of us could never come back from. Don't you ever apologize to me. Got it?"

I nodded, and then wiped my tears away.

Nicky pulled my comforter back and helped me into bed, saying she would wake me for dinner. Pulling the covers up to my chin, I began to drift off, praying for a dreamless sleep.

***

Lying on a dirty concrete floor, I quickly took in my dimly lit surroundings. I was back in the basement of Francis Medley's home. He was standing near his torture table, carefully running his fingers along each knife, and humming a tune to himself.

Why was I here again? I wasn't chained to the wall as I had been but lying on the cold dank floor. The bastard must have thought I'd passed out from blood loss and removed my restraints. *His mistake.* I assessed my major injuries: one stab wound to the leg, one to the shoulder, and a deep slice in my gut. They hurt like a bitch, but I sucked up the pain, knowing I had to find a way to safety.

Forming a plan in my mind, I decided to act as if I was still unconscious, and when the time was right, I would strike. Keeping my eyes closed, I listened to the sound of Francis's breathing when he stopped humming. His footsteps drawing ever nearer, I could hear the soles of his shoes pounding against the concrete. It sounded like an echo reverberating in my head.

Sweat began to form along my brow, knowing my time was coming. It was kill or be killed, that much I knew; my backup would never come. When I felt his hot breath near my skin, my eyes snapped open, and I reached up with both hands, wrapping them around his throat with strength I didn't know I had.

Francis's eyes bulged in what looked like fear and surprise. "You shouldn't have unchained me, you sick son of a bitch. You're gonna die tonight." I peered into his watery brown eyes, so he could see my icy blue stare. I wanted the last thing he saw to be my face—the face of the woman he'd assaulted. The woman he'd tried to murder.

No. That wasn't good enough. I sat up as he struggled against my grip; he had dropped his knife, and I quickly snatched it after freeing one hand from his throat.

He sucked in a ragged breath. "You will not win, Charlotte. This is all a game of my making, and you, my dear, are just the victim." His words came out in raspy breaths as he gasped for air.

Choking him harder, pressing on his Adam's apple, I brought the knife to his throat. "No, Francis. That's where you're wrong. You fucked with the wrong woman this time." I pressed the knife firmly against his throat, watching as blood trickled down his neck from the small cut.

For a split-second, fear flashed across his face before it evolved into an evil sneer. "Get on with it then, little birdie. I'll always have your mother's delightful screams to live on with me for all eternity."

Fury and blind rage assaulted me. I reared up, slamming Francis onto the concrete floor, banging his head as hard as I could, and straddled his torso. "This is for my mother!" I brought the knife down quick and hard, stabbing him in the heart. Then continued to thrust the knife into his body repeatedly until I had no strength left within me. Blood sprayed across my face, and I relished it—the blood of the man who'd harmed me and murdered my parents.

He was dead, and I had killed him. Francis Medley could never harm another.

I stood, holding my middle, and began to limp away toward the basement stairs, then everything disappeared into pitch blackness.

***

I awoke screaming, soaked in sweat from head to toe. Nicky rushed into my bedroom, eyes wide with concern, and sat on my bed. "Char, what's going on? Are you all right?" She brushed my sweaty black mane away from my face.

"It was just a dream, that's all." My words were shaky, and tears trickled down my face.

I had killed Francis in my dream; it was so vivid and felt so real. How could I explain that to Nicky, let alone to myself? Sure, I wanted the piece of shit to die, but he needed to be prosecuted, regardless of my earlier thoughts. It was just how things worked, and there was enough evidence stacked against him, he would surely go down for his crimes.

"Char, that was not just any dream, hon. I heard you screaming and saying, 'die, you sick son of a bitch.' What can I do? I know you said you didn't want to talk about it, but maybe you should."

She placed her hand on my face, wiping away a few stray tears, and looking as if she was about to cry. This was not the Nicky I knew. Emotion? Where was this coming from? Oh, me. Clearly, she was worried, *and* she cared. Thank God for her.

I mustered the courage I really didn't have at the time. "Well, how about we look over my staples, and you help me into the shower. Some coffee might do me good, and then maybe we can talk, okay? That dream scared the shit out of me."

"All right, hon. Whatever you need." She pulled the covers back and helped me to stand, then led me to the bathroom, turning the knob to let the hot water flow from the shower.

"Thank you, Nicky. You don't know how much this means to me—you being here, helping me. I don't know what I'd do without you."

I allowed the tears to fall once more. I couldn't have held them back if I tried. That damn dream, and then the thought of having to make burial arrangements for my mom and dad tomorrow popped into my head. I wanted to vomit.

Undressing and stepping into the steaming hot shower, I allowed the water to flow over my body, washing away the remnants of the nightmare. Careful of my injuries, stitches, and the plastic bandage covering the staples in my stomach, I cleaned my body the best I could, and attempted to wash my hair. Sort of. It would have to do.

Nicky was waiting for me with towels in hand when I stepped out. The woman was wonderful. She turned her head to give me privacy, but helped when I needed it, even wrapping a towel around my wet hair because I couldn't raise my arms high enough to get it just right.

The little things are always what we take for granted.

After she'd redressed my wounds, and I was clothed in loose-fitting shorts and a huge shirt, I walked to my small dining room situated to the left of my small galley kitchen and took a seat at my four-person cherry wood table. Nicky had a large carafe of coffee waiting for me, with freshly baked bran muffins sitting on a cooling rack.

Who knew she was Betty Crocker? I was learning a lot about my friend today. I shook my head and smiled, pouring myself a steaming cup of black coffee and placing a muffin on the plate Nicky had set out for me.

I tried not to look at the angry red stitched-up slash marks that would soon be scars on the top of my hands.

After a few minutes, she joined me in the dining room. "Who says a girl can't have dessert before dinner? It's bullshit anyway." She smiled, snatching a muffin from the rack, taking a large bite.

"You're the best. This is all too much. I had no idea you were such a homemaker." I raised a brow in question with a slight smirk.

"Oh, don't give me that. Just because I sling booze, doesn't mean my mamma didn't teach me right. Of course, I can cook."

"Speaking of booze, how about a drink later tonight? I'm not taking those painkillers the doctor prescribed me. So, why not?"

I needed a drink, not a painkiller knocking me out. I was afraid if I went back to sleep, I'd have another nightmare.

Nicky gave me a questioning look. "You sure? I mean, do you think... Oh, what the hell? I'll grab some from the bar later, but right now, I think we need to have a little chat."

I sighed and took a sip of my coffee. "I know we do, but I need to ask you something first. Will you take me to Brooks Funeral Home, so I can make arrangements for my parents' caskets tomorrow, around two?"

"You don't even need to ask, Char. That's what I'm here for. I have Johnny running the bar until I come back. I'm all yours."

I nodded and set my coffee cup on the table. "All right then. I also need to contact the priest at Saint Williams." I let out a breath. "I haven't talked to Father Paul in years. I'm not sure I can do this, Nicky."

Nicky stood from her chair and knelt by my side, taking my hands in hers. "Char, you're not alone in this. I'll be with you every step of the way. I know your heart hurts, but I'm here. Cry, scream, throw shit—I don't care. Whatever it takes, okay?"

I bobbed my head, not wanting to cry anymore. The truth was, I hadn't stepped foot in my family's church in nearly three years.

Again, I was *too busy*. What would Father Paul think of me now that my parents were dead? Would he blame me, too?

No. I needed to stop. He was a man of God who had always been there for me, even as a child, alone and broken when my adoptive parents had taken me in. Father Paul knew me. If anything, he would help me get through my grief, and most importantly, my guilt.

"Thank you, Nicky. For everything." I looked at her with tears welling behind my eyes. I honestly couldn't thank her enough; she was all I had left—I had no living relatives.

I wasn't used to being cared for like this, except by my mother when I was younger. That thought hurt to think about. I had never felt so helpless.

"What are friends for?" She smiled, patting my knee, and then walked to the kitchen to grab plates for the spaghetti she'd cooked while I was sleeping. "Now we eat, and you talk. I honestly think it'll make you feel a bit better."

I sighed again, looking at my plate of spaghetti. It smelled delicious, and I was starving. Twisting a few noodles with small meatballs around my fork, I took a bite. My stomach attempted to protest, even though it tasted amazing. My nerves were getting the best of me.

I set my fork on the table and looked at Nicky. I began by telling her how I'd heard the call on the radio about Francis Medley and went from there. Technically, I wasn't supposed to divulge information about an ongoing case, but at that point, and after what that psychotic piece of shit had done to me, I had no shits to give. I also knew she would take what I told her to her grave.

Open mouthed and in shock, Nicky had tears rolling down her face once I'd finished. "I knew it was bad, Char, but I had no idea as to what extent. He was stalking your mom and dad, too? This whole time?" She slammed her fork onto the table. Her blue eyes were wild and angry. "I wanna kill the son of a bitch myself!"

"Now you know why I had the nightmare. Mom's face. I can't get it out of my head, Nicky. And what he did to my dad? Shit like that you can't unsee. I have no one left." I began sobbing into my hands and felt the staples in my stomach give a little. I had to lean back in my chair so as to not bust another one. I did *not* want to go back to the damn hospital.

Nicky reached across the table, pulling my hands down, as tears continued to fall down her face. "You'll always have me. We may not be blood, but you're my sister in every way. You hear me? You are *not* alone. I've got you. I'm not going anywhere."

We cried for several minutes, until Nicky had had enough. "All right. It's booze time. No more of this crying shit today. We're gonna drown our sorrows, chick. We can cry tomorrow." She wiped her face with the back of her sleeve and winked at me.

I had to laugh and agree.

"I'm calling Johnny now and having someone bring us some tequila. Margarita night!" She jumped up, and danced around the table, shaking her ass. That girl was crazy as a loon, and that's why I loved her so much. Even during the absolute worst moment of my life, she could still make me smile.

Chapter 6

Margarita night turned out to be a sob fest. I knew better than to drink when my emotions were in turmoil. I only had one drink and decided that was enough. Nicky was amazing; she listened to me howl all night long. Once I started talking, it was like the dam had broken, and I couldn't stop. I continued seeing the battered faces of my mom and dad flash in my mind, breaking me even further.

I wanted Francis Medley to pay. Not only for murdering my parents, but for murdering all of those other women, too. I was lucky. I had survived, albeit not unharmed, but I was alive and breathing. That much, I was grateful for. The rest, I knew I would have to take one day at a time.

Nicky and I even broached the topic of me having to go to trial as a witness. At that, I broke down, having a panic attack out of nowhere at the mere thought of seeing his miserable face again. I knew then, something had to give. The captain and the damn doctor were right: I was going to have to speak to a therapist. I couldn't process these emotions alone. But first things first, I had to bury my parents.

After a long night of Nicky drinking margaritas, and me pouring my heart out, we finally made it to bed around two a.m. I fell asleep in no time at all.

***

I was there again, lying on the basement floor, but it was different. I could see the knife not too far from me, where Francis had dropped it when I'd rammed his balls into his throat. My body hurt like hell, but the glint of the knife reflecting from the dim lighting gave me hope.

I glanced to the side, seeing Francis standing in front of his torture table, not making a sound. He had no idea I was awake. As soundlessly as I could, I moved a little to left, grasping the knife in my left hand; he was only about a foot away now.

I could hear him breathing, and knew I only had one chance to make my move, or I would die just like his other victims. Strengthening my resolve, and sucking up the pain, I inched closer, until the back of his legs were just within striking distance.

With one swing of the knife, I sliced both of his Achilles tendons, knocking him to the floor. I turned quickly, to remove myself from the path of his fall. Francis yelped out in pain, glancing around to find the person who'd attacked him.

I carefully sat up, clutching my middle, and scooted closer, so he could see my face clearly. "You should have killed me when you had the chance, you sadistic son of a bitch."

Without warning, I slammed the knife into his stomach before he could make a move, and he cried out again. This time, he looked into my eyes.

"Your father squealed like a pig. Kill me," he rasped, "but your beloved parents are still *dead*."

I saw red. I drew up to my knees, forgetting my pain, and stabbed him in the face, then his heart, and continued to thrust the knife until his blood covered every inch of my body, mixing with my own.

***

When the alarm sounded at nine, I wanted to scream. My head pounded like I had a freakin' hangover from hell, but it was from crying all night long. I just knew my eyes were even more swollen. I didn't want to look at myself in the mirror.

I pulled the covers back, being careful of my wounds—I was in even more pain than before—and slowly walked to my bathroom. I turned on the faucet to splash cold water on my face, but when I looked down at my hands, I saw blood.

My hands were covered in *blood*, and not mine—my sutures were intact all the way up to the gashes on my arms. I screamed at the top of lungs, trembling from head to toe. This had to be another nightmare, or I was losing my mind altogether. I ran my hands furiously beneath the stream of water, forgetting the stitches, but nothing happened. I kept blinking, trying to make it all go away.

Nicky rushed into the bathroom like a madwoman. "Char! What the hell? Are you okay? I thought you had fallen." She was out of breath when she reached for me.

I held up my trembling hands. "Blood. It's everywhere. It won't wash off." And the waterworks started again. I couldn't control the sobs that escaped me. Would I ever be normal again?

"Char, honey, your hands are fine. There's no blood." She looked into the basin. "There's none in the sink, either. I think you were dreaming again."

When I looked down at my hands, the blood was gone, only those godforsaken stitches—a sick reminder of what had happened to me. I was losing my fucking mind. "But it was there—I saw it." *Did I imagine it?* I thought to myself. "Forget it. You're right. I didn't sleep well." I released a measured breath, attempting to stop the flow of tears. "I think it's because of what I have to do today."

Then, I remembered the nightmare. Oh, God. Not again. Why was this happening?

Nicky hugged me gently. "I'm here, and you don't have to worry. We'll get through this together, all right?" She released me and looked into my eyes. "Let's get you dressed."

I could only nod, and then I blindly walked back into my room. I knew what I'd seen, but that didn't make a damn bit of difference if it wasn't real. I planned on talking to Father Paul about it later. I'd experienced similar things after my birthparents were murdered: hearing gunshots and seeing pools of blood that weren't there. He'd helped me then, and I was certain he could help me now. I'd have to talk to him about the dreams, too. This had to stop.

Nicky had borrowed some of her younger brother's clothes, so I would be more comfortable. My jeans and T-shirts, or even work clothes, just wouldn't work with my body in the state that it was.

Once I was dressed in loose-fitting jogging pants, that I had to roll down at the waist, and a large shirt—I looked like I was wearing my father's clothes. *I will not cry.* I went to the dining room table where Nicky had set out a carafe of coffee with two mugs. I poured myself a cup and sat down, waiting for her to get ready.

My cell phone vibrated on the coffee table in the living room, adjacent to the dining room from where I was sitting. Although it was only a few feet away, I knew it would feel like a mile's walk. I huffed, and then walked over to pick up the phone. It was Greg.

"Hello, Greg."

"Hey, Char. I'm sorry to bother you, but me and Stephanie need to ask you a few questions about...that night with Francis."

"Are you fucking kidding me?" I couldn't believe today of all days they wanted a statement. Why hadn't they asked for it while I was in the hospital?

"I know it's not ideal, but we wanted to give you time to rest and allow some of your memories to return before we took your statement. You know it's only a formality." I could hear the frustration in his voice.

"I know this, Greg, but today is *not* a good day. I'm making arrangements for my parents, for God's sake!"

He sighed into the phone. "I wouldn't ask if I didn't have to, and you know that."

I breathed deeply, attempting to rein in my anger. "You have ten fucking minutes. I have to be at the funeral home by two this afternoon, and it's now eleven. I suggest you hurry the hell up."

I hung up on him, ending the call. And Stephanie Hamilton of all people? The one detective I could barely stand the sight of? I hoped I could get through this interview without snapping at her.

Stephanie and I had a history. She was the type who always attempted to throw her good looks around to get what she wanted, giving all women in our profession a bad name. It had never set well with me. As a detective, you got by on your merits and your ability to do excellent police work, not batting your eyelashes and shaking your ass.

I'd tried talking to her on several occasions, but she would never listen to me. I was never nasty toward her, only tried to boost her confidence in ways that proved she didn't have to act like a fool, without saying as much. I was a bitch, but not *that* bad. I truly wanted her to succeed.

Stephanie was a damned good detective; I just wished *she* could see it that way. I hoped she would soon learn using her feminine charm would not get her very far, not in the way she wanted.

Nicky must have heard me shouting. She walked into the living room, towel-drying her hair. "What was that all about?"

I went back to my now-cold coffee. "Greg and Hamilton want my statement about that night."

"Are you shittin' me? Now?"

"Nope. Not one shit." I refreshed my cup of coffee. "They'll be here soon, and I only gave them ten minutes."

She slid into her chair and poured herself a cup of coffee. "All right. Do you want me in here with you when they come?"

"If you want. You can keep me from strangling Hamilton." I smiled evilly. "We never really got along, and I'm assuming she's Greg's new interim partner."

"Alrighty then. I'll hurry up and get dressed." She swigged her coffee, stood from the table, and went back to the bathroom to finish getting ready.

Fifteen minutes later, a loud knock sounded at the door, breaking me from my thoughts of that damned nightmare and coffee-induced haze. I knew it was them, and all of a sudden, my heart tried to break free from the confines of my chest.

I didn't want to talk about this shit but knew it was necessary. Sure, I'd given Greg a hard time, mostly out of self-preservation, and also because I needed a clear head when I went to the funeral home. It seemed that wasn't going to happen today.

I opened the door to see Stephanie standing in front with her blonde hair hanging in waves, blue eyes sparkling, and what looked like a fake smile splitting her face. Why the hell was she smiling? What was there to smile about?

"Hey, Char," Stephanie said, extending her right hand, "how are you?"

Was she insane? I looked down at my own hands covered in stitches, and raised them for her to see, without shaking hers in return.

"Come in." That was all the "pleasantries" she was going to receive from me after that.

Maybe she was nervous. I realized I was being a bitch and needed to lighten up a bit.

Stephanie's smile fell, and she nodded politely, then Greg followed her, looking grim. "Hey, Char. Sorry about today." He walked past me and looked around. "Do you care if we sit down?"

"No, Greg. You have to stand the entire time... Of course, you can sit." I gestured toward the couch with a strained smile.

Damn. I really *was* being a bitch and needed to tone it down a bit. The nightmare had set me off, and it wasn't their fault.

He shook his head and smiled back, taking a seat on my sofa. Stephanie sat next to him. I sat in the brown leather chair opposite them, near the doors leading to the balcony.

"First, I'd like to say I'm sorry," Greg began. "I know how difficult this must be for you after everything, so we'll keep this brief.

"I just need to know how you ended up"— he cleared his throat—"in the basement. We heard your call for backup but were detained by a robbery-homicide."

So that was it, why they hadn't come. It still didn't answer as to why they hadn't sent uniformed officers to the scene. I attempted to keep a straight face to mask my anger toward them and at my own stupidity for going in alone.

"As you know, I heard the call and asked for backup. I knew exactly where he was and didn't want to run the risk of him making a run for it."

Flashbacks of his filthy living room, boxes stacked against the walls, and the smell of rotten food assaulted my mind. I went in as I had been trained to do, checking each disgusting room, making sure they were clear, with my hand on my weapon at all times, never leaving my back open.

"And, your weapon—how did Francis remove it from you?"

I took a deep breath, attempting to reel in the memories, and my emotions. "He was hiding in a makeshift passageway after I'd deemed the living room secure. I didn't see him, and he knocked me out.

"The next thing I knew, I was hanging from chains in his basement, waiting for backup that never arrived." I eyeballed him, and then Stephanie, who looked a bit green. She was staring at my face and arms. "So, there you have it. I woke up in the hospital after he'd tortured, and nearly killed me. Are we done here?"

Greg was taking notes as I spoke. I wondered if he wrote down the part where they'd let me down and left me to die.

"Did Francis say anything in particular, anything that stands out..."

I didn't know if I'd answered his question; I was somewhere else. My heart was beating frantically now. I could see Francis's face clearly in my mind, and I thought I was going to be sick. The knife against my face, slicing my gut, and then stabbing me. I could feel it. I was there again. I had no oxygen left to breathe.

The walls were slowly closing in on me; my ears were ringing, and my mother's battered face flashed before my eyes. I wanted to scream but couldn't; I had no voice, no air. Beady brown eyes hovered in my consciousness, roving over my body, my death clearly in his stare. I was helpless to fight back.

"Sing, little birdie," played over and over in my head. His voice like rough sandpaper, a constant buzzing in my ears that I couldn't escape. Still, I couldn't scream. I knew I was going to die.

My mother's face became my own, lying on a cold slab. I felt what she felt: death, all-consuming. I was gone.

Darkness consumed me, and I felt myself hit the floor.

Chapter 7

"Char! Wake up, honey." Nicky's hand gently patted my face. I could hear panic in her voice, but it was so far away. Everything was so far away...

The buzzing in my ears was slowly fading, but the pain in my chest was still there. I could barely breathe. I wanted to open my eyes, but I was afraid of what I might see.

"Come on, Char, open your eyes." Nicky's voice was closer now. I could hear other voices, too. And then shouting.

"What the fuck did you say to her, Greg?" That was Nicky. "You just couldn't wait, could you? You know what kind of hell she's been through, and what she has to do today. As if losing her parents wasn't enough, you fuckers come in here and do this!"

I opened my eyes.

Nicky was standing now with her finger pointed directly in Greg's face. Stephanie was backed away near the balcony doors. If I weren't in so much pain, and freaked the hell out, it might have been a little funny. A little...

Only because Nicky was scaring the bejeezus out of them.

"That's enough," I choked out. My breathing was still ragged.

"Char! You had another panic attack." Nicky ran to my side. "Do you need anything? Are your stitches all right? Are you bleeding?" She frantically looked over my body.

"Nicky. Stop." That was a lot of questions. "Just help me up, gently please." Damn. I'd fallen hard, and my body hurt like hell.

"Let me help," Greg offered.

"No." Nicky pushed him away. "You and your *friend* have done enough!"

Stephanie's eyes bulged, but she didn't say a word. She hadn't said anything at all since they'd arrived. I wondered if it was my appearance that shocked her, or if she just didn't know what to say. I honestly felt bad for her, even if we weren't on the best of terms.

Greg backed off with his hands raised. "I'm sorry, Char. I had no idea—I…just didn't know this would happen."

"Now you do," Nicky snapped, pointing toward the door. "Get the hell out of her apartment. You can talk to her later. She'll sign your statement some other time."

"I'll call you, Greg," I said, still somewhat out of breath, when Nicky helped me to sit in the chair.

He looked like a kicked puppy, and shook his head, then Stephanie followed him out of the door, closing it behind them.

"Are you sure you're all right?" Nicky was still looking me over from head to toe, checking for bleeding.

"Yes, I'm fine, just another panic attack. I keep seeing him, and my mother. This time, I was my mom and felt her death. God, Nicky. It was so real." I tried not to cry. I decided to keep the nightmare to myself for now.

She plopped down on the floor next to my chair. "Shit. I know you don't want to hear this again right now, but you really need to talk to someone. This isn't good, Char. Not at all. I mean, I can listen, but I'm no good with advice, other than wanting to kill the bastard myself."

I sighed heavily, attempting to erase the horrific images I'd seen in my panic-stricken mind. "I know that now. It's just a matter of when."

Nicky patted my leg, looking up at me. "You scared the shit out of me. I hate this for you and wish there was more I could do, help take some of it away." She folded her hands in her lap and took a deep breath. I knew she was trying to hide her emotions. "Look, we'll do what we can with the burial arrangements today, and then I think you should go and talk to your priest, and not just about the funeral services."

"I was thinking the same. I can't continue on like this, afraid to close my eyes, or even talk about what happened." I attempted to stop more tears from falling, but my mother's face kept flashing into the forefront of my mind. "I realize it's only been a short time, and I haven't had time to process it all just yet, but something has to give."

Nicky stood and made me a cup of coffee, then brought it over to me. "This probably isn't the best for your nerves, but I know how much you like it." She tried to smile and failed.

I felt like such a burden, helpless to care for myself as I always had in the past. But inside, I knew I was stronger than this. I had

78

never been a woman to cower in fear, and I just needed to pull myself together—somehow. My injuries being a constant reminder didn't help much, but I was determined to make it through.

I knew by allowing fear to rule my every waking moment, I was giving the person who'd harmed me power he didn't deserve. I didn't even want to say his name. I had *lived*, and I needed to be grateful for that; so many others had not. Regardless of what I had to endure, I'd stopped him from harming another.

My wounds would heal; the scars would remind me that I was a survivor, *not* a victim. Now, I just needed the rest of my brain to get on board.

I accepted the warm cup. "Thank you, Nicky." After taking a sip, I continued. "We should probably call Brooks and see if we can come in a little earlier. I just want to pick out something beautiful for Mamma, and Dad." My heart broke a little again thinking about them. "Then we can head over to St. Williams and speak with Father Paul. I know he's expecting me."

"All right, hon. Whatever you need to do, but are you sure you're okay? I mean, you still look a bit pale." She looked down at my hands. "Let me see them. I think you may have opened a stitch or two. I'm not sure you're supposed to get those wet or scrub them like you did."

I groaned, setting my coffee cup on the side table, and showed her my hands. "They'll be fine, I'm more worried about my gut than anything. As long as the staples don't bust, I'm good."

"Stubborn ass." Nicky dropped my hands back in my lap. "Whatever you say. I'll call Brooks Funeral Home now and see if we can leave."

"Thank you." I looked past her, staring out of the patio doors, looking onto the crowded street. I was going to be normal again, come hell or high water. I just needed to make it through the next few days.

***

Brooks Funeral Home was more than accommodating. The receptionist told Nicky we could come when we were ready. It was only a fifteen-minute drive to Canal Street, so it wouldn't take that long if traffic permitted.

It was a hell of a trek down those damn stairs, and by the time we made it to her car in our parking lot, I felt like I was going to pass out. I wondered how long it was going to take for my body to heal. This sucked!

Nicky helped me into the car, and I put on a pair of huge sunglasses. No need in scaring people with my appearance when we made our way to the funeral home.

The drive over was silent. I didn't have much to say and thought about what my mom and dad would want. I knew they had an insurance policy to cover their burial expenses, but I had yet to look into it. I did know it was something the funeral home could help me with. I would have to contact our family attorney after everything was sorted out.

When we arrived in the parking lot, I looked at the beautiful, two-story white home that had been converted into a place where loved ones were able to say their last goodbyes. My heart stuck in my throat. I knew I was only picking out their caskets, but this was something I'd never thought about, especially at twenty-seven.

I sucked up my courage and steeled my nerves. Nicky walked around to the passenger side and helped me to my feet, closing the door behind her. I felt myself falling into despair again the closer we walked toward the main entrance, but I pushed my emotions down. I had to be strong for my parents; they deserved more from me. I could do this.

As I walked into the lobby, my mouth nearly dropped open. It was ornately decorated with Victorian furniture and polished cherry wood tables, bringing on a sense of calm. Soft music played in the background, and I felt myself sigh in relief. I wasn't sure what I had expected.

"Hello, you must be Charlotte," the receptionist greeted me with a smile. She didn't offer to shake my hand, and I was grateful. She was a beautiful African American woman whose kindness shone in her honey-colored eyes, dressed modestly in a navy-blue blazer, matching skirt, and a white silk blouse.

"Yes, thank you for moving up my appointment." I glanced around again at my surroundings. "I really appreciate it." I took a deep breath and exhaled. I could do this.

She gestured for me and Nicky to sit in the two mahogany leather chairs opposite her desk. "It was no bother at all. My name is Alexandria, but you can call me Alex."

"This is Nicky; she'll be with me through all of this. I hope that's okay." I had no idea what the formalities were in cases such as this.

"Nice to meet you, Nicky," she said, shaking her hand and then taking a seat behind her desk, "and yes,"—she looked toward me—"you can bring along anyone you need during this time."

"Thank you. I'm in need of a casket—two caskets." I nearly broke down but contained myself. "Services will be held at St. Williams Catholic Church."

"Yes, yes, we've worked with them on many occasions," Alex said. "Would you like to see our casket room now? We can work out the paperwork later."

Not another panic attack. I could feel it coming on. I slowly began breathing in through my nose and out through my mouth. I felt Nicky place her hand on mine. I would be all right. I had to be.

"Please. I would like that." Nicky helped me to stand, and we walked to the back room where caskets lined all four walls.

I stopped in the entryway, seeing casket upon casket. I didn't know what to do. I felt Nicky beside me, and all I could do was stare open-mouthed. I heard Alex talking to me, but her voice seemed like background noise. There were just so many. What if I picked the wrong one? What if... And, oh, God—the headstone. I hadn't thought about that.

83

"Nicky, I can't do this. I need you to take over from here. I just... can't." Fighting back tears, I turned away from the room and stood in the hallway, leaned against the wall, attempting to catch my breath.

Nicky stood before me and looked directly into my eyes. "Char, you don't have a choice. You have to do this. I know it's hard, but breathe. Let's walk in there together and pick out their caskets."

"Headstones, Nicky." I couldn't say much else. "They need headstones, too."

"All right. Then we'll order those as well. I just need you to be the Charlotte I know you are: strong and take-no-shit. You may not feel like her right now, but she's still in there."

I nodded my head, knowing she was right. If I didn't do this, who would? I needed to get my shit together. Fear—heartbreak: two things that I was allowing to control me. Dammit! I would *not* break.

I walked back into the dreaded room where Alex awaited me. She looked as if she understood. I was certain she'd seen her share of distraught family members. I glanced around to the far-left wall seeing only black caskets. No. Absolutely not. My mother would come back and haunt me for burying her in black.

Nicky and I walked farther back, while Alex stood to the side, and then I saw it. A pearl-white casket, trimmed in delicate pink roses, just like Mamma would have wanted. White satin filled the interior. I pointed, and Nicky told Alex it was the one I wanted. I hadn't quite found my voice yet, but I would.

Alex jotted everything down on her notepad and then followed us to the right side of the room. I knew my dad would want something with chrome, manly with no flowers, or any kind of decorative crap. I could hear him in my head at the thought of putting him in the exact same casket as my mom. I laughed a little at that.

I was finally calming down, feeling my parents near me, if only in my mind. I found a polished mahogany casket, with chrome handles, and knew it would fit my father perfectly.

After we were finished with everything, Alex led us into what looked like a conference room. She brought a book with her that I assumed was for headstones. I breathed deeply again and took my seat in one of the high-back leather chairs.

It was a lot easier than I thought. I found a double, heart-shaped, black granite headstone—perfect for them—and told her

85

what I wanted engraved: *Loving parents of Charlotte Pierce. Gone but not forgotten.* I was going to send her a picture of the two of them to be placed in the center.

Alex informed me she would get all the necessary paperwork from our family attorney, Jack Flanigan, and send the caskets to St. Williams once she discussed the details with Father Paul's secretary, Nancy. She said she would also recover and prepare their remains. I zoned out when she discussed that part. I knew it would be a closed-casket funeral.

After signing the necessary paperwork, I thanked Alex for her kindness and patience, then Nicky and I left without incident. I was finally okay. Well, as okay as I could be.

Next on the agenda was setting the date of the funeral with Father Paul.

Chapter 8

When we arrived outside of Saint Williams Catholic Church, a feeling of peace washed over me, something I hadn't felt since I was a child. I could feel the presence of God; it was strange. I'd thought maybe He had left me a long time ago, but being back here, in my family's church, I felt like a child again. Safe.

The cathedral was small, built of brown brick, and the steeple, or bell tower, held a large church bell that I'd always enjoyed looking at when my parents would stand outside, congregating with fellow parishioners after Mass. A statue of the Virgin Mary was centered off to the left, with a large fountain surrounding her. The wooden double-doored entrance was welcoming, just as I had remembered.

When Nicky and I were walking toward the doors, Father Paul walked out to greet us. He was dressed in his typical black priest attire, with a white collar. Standing around five-feet-ten inches tall, he had grown a short beard since I'd seen him last, and his snow-white hair was trimmed short.

"Charlotte, my dear child, I'm so sorry for your loss." He hugged me gently, careful not to hurt me—my wounds were clearly visible. "Come, come. Let's go inside." He looked toward my friend, his kind blue eyes misting with unshed tears. "And you must be Nicky. I've heard a lot about you." He reached out and grasped her hand. "Welcome. Thank you for taking care of our girl. You're a kind soul."

Nicky shook his hand in return, smiled, and then followed us inside the cathedral.

Memories of my childhood came rushing forth when I stepped inside the church; nothing had changed. I remembered Mamma singing in the choir, while Dad and I sat in the right front pew; her voice was beautiful and melodic. She used to sing me to sleep when I had nightmares as a child. I would miss her voice.

Fifteen rows of wooden pews lined each side, with stained-glass windows depicting the stations of the cross every few feet along the walls. The painted cathedral ceiling portraying archangels could be seen above, a beautiful sight to behold, even now as an adult. The altar was situated in the middle of the room, where a large crucifix hung above it, with Blessed Mother on the left, and Saint Joseph on the right.

I pushed back the memories that threatened to take over my mind, so I could deal with what I had to do. "Thank you for having us, Father."

He nodded for us to follow him into his office located in the back. "I wouldn't have it any other way, Charlotte. Your family has always been a huge part of this congregation, and they will be sorely missed." He swiped an errant tear from his cheek.

Nicky and I followed him into his small office where books lined the walls, and a lone crucifix hung directly above his weathered wooden desk. He motioned for us to sit in the chairs opposite him.

We took our seats, and I inhaled a sharp breath. "I've made the necessary arrangements with Brooks Funeral home, and they should be contacting you shortly. I would like to set up"—I had to take another steady breath to calm my nerves—"the date for their Mass and funeral. There will be no viewing. Friends only."

I was straight and to the point. I didn't think I could say much else, and I didn't want to go into further detail. I'd held myself together for the most part and had no desire to break again.

"I understand," Father Paul agreed. "I will get with Nancy and ensure all arrangements are made to your specifications." He leaned forward, clasping his hands together. "The parish has put together a donation for all flower arrangements to be delivered when the time comes. Is there anything specific you want draped over their caskets?"

I heard Nicky sniffle beside me. I wanted to do the same, but only nodded, then said, "*Loving Mother*, and *Loving Father*, should do. And, thank you. I don't know what to say."

I couldn't believe the kindness of these people. The love and generosity they were showing toward my parents; it warmed my heart.

"We know a little of what you've been through, and no one wanted you to be burdened with the task of preparing it all yourself. We are a church family here. We care about you, Charlotte." He was so sincere, and my heart... I just couldn't...

"Father, if I may," Nicky said. "I think I'll step outside so Charlotte can speak with you in private."

Father Paul looked at her in question, then back to me. "All right. We have plenty of time."

Nicky excused herself, squeezed my shoulder, glancing at me with "the look," then turned and walked out of the door, closing it behind her.

I wasn't sure if I was ready for this talk just yet, but I knew Nicky was right. It needed to happen sooner rather than later, especially with burying my parents looming over me.

I sat forward a little in my chair and then looked down at my hands. "Father, do you remember the hallucinations and nightmares I had after my birthparents were killed?" I couldn't look at him, not yet.

"Yes, my child. I do. That's not something easily forgotten." He stood from his desk and came to sit next to me in the chair Nicky had just vacated. "Are the nightmares back?"

I straightened and looked at him. "Not about my birthparents, but about what happened to me. I'm having vivid dreams of killing the man who harmed me and murdered Mom and Dad. I'm afraid to go to sleep." I absently picked at the pants I was wearing. It was so much harder to say aloud.

"Charlotte, you've experienced a horrific trauma. This isn't uncommon; unsettling to the psyche, yes, but not uncommon." He looked toward the crucifix above his desk. "Have you prayed about it?"

I had to be honest here. I hadn't *really* prayed in years. "No. Not since I was younger. I'm having panic attacks, and seeing blood that isn't really there, just like before."

"If I remember correctly, you had similar episodes that went on for nearly a year after Dan and Leanne adopted you." He looked me directly in the eye. "You will have to find a way to deal with these emotions, cope with them somehow—find a productive outlet, and release the pain. It won't happen overnight. I would suggest finding a good counselor or psychiatrist who deals in this sort of thing.

"I believe what you're experiencing is post-traumatic stress disorder, but I'm not a doctor, Charlotte. While I'm always here to help you, there are medical professionals who are more adept in treating cases such as yours. I wish I could take it all away." His eyes were sad when he looked at me.

Well, I was hoping *he* could help me. I was guessing murdering my attacker in my dreams might have been out of his area of expertise, and I was no longer a child. I really didn't want to see a shrink, or even think about PTSD.

"Do you think I'll ever get back to normal? I can't continue to live like this, Father."

He gently touched my hand. "You are one of the strongest women I know. I have no doubt. I will suggest that you pray a little; it does help, you know." He gave me a half smile;

the same one he always did when I was a teenager.

"I'll do my best, Father. I'm just a little out of practice. Thank you for listening to me."

"Anytime, my dear. My door is always open to you, and I'm always here to listen when you need an ear."

I carefully stood, ending the meeting. "Will you please call me and let me know when Nancy has a date for the funeral?"

"Absolutely. Most likely this Friday, but I'll be in touch." He stood to hug me again. "Take good care of yourself, Charlotte, and may God bless you and heal you."

"Thank you, Father."

I turned and opened the door to find Nicky waiting for me in the rear pew. When she saw me, she stood, and then we left the church.

I felt a sense of relief, having talked with Father Paul, but I'd been hoping for a bit more. At least now the funeral preparations were made, and the worst part was over.

***

Services were held on Friday afternoon at two p.m., just as Father Paul had said. It rained that day. All I could think of was tears falling from Heaven. I was numb. I'd worn a long-sleeved, knee-length black dress to cover my wounds, and a floppy black hat with sunglasses. I didn't want to speak to anyone.

The Mass was beautiful, but I could barely concentrate, only seeing the caskets of my mother and father in front of me. Friends of theirs had come by offering their condolences, and all I could do was nod. Some may have thought me to be rude, but I honestly didn't care. I had Nicky by my side the entire time, and that was all that mattered. She was my anchor. I just needed to get through this day.

When it came time for the burial, there was a white tent erected above their graves. I wasn't sure who had chosen the pallbearers, but I was grateful. Nicky produced an umbrella as the rain descended upon us. I felt like I was in a living nightmare; that this wasn't really happening—I couldn't possibly be burying my parents.

Out of the corner of my eye, I saw half of the New Orleans Homicide Department pulling onto the gravel road in unmarked Crown Vic's and then walking toward the grave site; my heart shuddered in my chest. They didn't have to come. I hadn't even invited them. As a matter of fact, I'd treated them all like shit. The fact that they were here made me realize that they did care, and maybe I was just overreacting because of everything I had been through.

Greg was the first to greet me, followed by Captain Davis. "We love you," Greg said with emotion in his voice. "I hope you know that."

My arms were folded against my chest, and all I could do was nod in response to my shock of them being here.

"Char, I meant what I said before," Captain Davis said. "We're here for you."

I thanked them both and then turned back to the pallbearers. It was almost time.

Nicky cleared her throat and said hello to Greg. I was surprised she didn't punch him, but it really wasn't the time or the place.

When it was time for everyone to gather around the caskets, I took my seat, and Nicky sat next to me. Father Paul began to pray, and again, I tuned out, thinking of precious memories long forgotten with my mom and dad.

I smiled to myself when I remembered our first time at the beach. Mamma had decided it was "high time I saw the 'real' ocean"—her words. I had finally stopped having nightmares, and she wanted me to have a slice of normalcy. They'd taken me to Key West. I remembered the beautiful white sand squishing between my tiny toes like it was yesterday. It had been the first time since losing my birthparents that I'd truly felt happy, and genuinely loved.

We'd made sandcastles, and Dad let Mom and me bury him in sand up to his neck. I remembered laughing when Mamma threw seawater all over him, making the sand even heavier. Instead of getting angry, Dad only laughed, and then sprung from the sand like a zombie, chasing us down the shoreline. It was one of my greatest memories. After that, Mom and Dad decided we'd make an annual trip to the Keys during summer vacation.

I knew then, that if I held these memories close to my heart, my parents would never truly be gone. They would live on with me until the day I died.

Father Paul's voice broke me from my thoughts. It was time to lay the white lilies across the caskets and say my final goodbyes. I felt like I just had. My heart was full of love, and yes, sadness, but I had finally let them go in my own way.

Nicky helped me to stand, and I walked toward their caskets, leaving my lilies on each one. I kissed my fingers and touched their coffins, whispering, "Until we meet again. I love you, Mom and Dad."

With that, I was ready to go. I didn't want to stick around for the food, or to talk to anyone. I had made my peace and knew my parents were no longer suffering. They were in my heart, where they would stay.

Chapter 9

Three weeks passed in a blur, and I was finally feeling a bit more like myself again. Nicky had taken me to the doctor to have my staples and stitches removed. Still the same orders: no heavy lifting, and to watch for any visible signs of infection. It was an ugly sight, but again, wounds healed, and even the ugly red scars would soon fade against my dark skin.

I was still on paid medical leave from the department, and Captain Davis had ordered mandatory counseling. I'd already told him I no longer wanted to work for NOPD Homicide, but he was having none of it, telling me to give my body time to properly heal first, then come back and talk to him. He wouldn't even accept my letter of resignation.

I'd always wanted to be a detective, but now, I just needed a change. It wasn't that I was giving up on life, just the opposite. I craved something less exciting, more low key for now. I had a lot to deal with, and I didn't think I could do my best work with everything I had on my plate. And I honestly wanted nothing more to do with homicide, not after what had happened.

The nightmares were still occurring, but less frequently now, and I continued to think about what Father Paul had said. I knew I couldn't just bury my emotions; one could never bury anything alive, it would always come back—ten times worse. Which brought me back to the counseling Captain Davis had ordered. Maybe it wouldn't hurt, but I would I have to think about it. I wasn't exactly fond of police-ordered shrinks.

Nicky was still staying with me, and occasionally working at The Styx, only at my insistence. I needed some alone time. Not that I didn't love her being here, but now that I was finally feeling better, and able to do more for myself, I wanted to do just that.

I'd decided I wanted a part-time job, and The Styx was the perfect place. When Nicky walked through the door, I paused the TV, and just stared at her from my perch on the couch.

"What? Do I smell?" She raised her arm, sniffing her armpit. I had to stifle a laugh.

"Um, no. I just wanted to talk to you, silly."

"Oh, okay. Why do you look so weird?" She was raising a brow, making an odd face.

"Just sit down. Good grief, woman." I laughed at her. "I just wanna ask you a question."

"All right," she dragged out, setting her purse on the dining room table, and then sat next to me on the couch. "What's this about?"

"Well, I wanna work part-time at The Styx, and before you say no, hear me out." I held up my hand before she could cut me off. "The department won't even let me quit, and I know I'm supposed to be taking it easy, so why not just a few days a week to see how I do?"

Nicky's mouth was open, most likely in shock. "Well, I mean, are you sure you're up for it?" She looked me up and down like a mother hen. "You just had your staples removed a week ago."

I let out a frustrated sigh. "Yes. I won't do any heavy lifting, and I'll be careful. I just wanna get outta this apartment and be around people. I'm sick of sitting around, watching my ass grow wider because you keep feeding me."

Nicky laughed. "Your ass is not fat. But, all right. You can start tomorrow night. Wednesday's aren't too busy, and you can work with me." She pointed her finger in my direction. "If I see you trying to lift anything heavy, I'm sending you home, though. I don't wanna have to take your stubborn ass back to the hospital, got it?"

"Yes, ma'am." I mock saluted her with a smile.

"Oh, before I forget, this came for you in the mail"—she stood and grabbed something from her purse, then handed me a large orange envelope—"but was delivered to my apartment; it looks like it's from your attorney."

Shit. It was from Jack Flanigan. I wondered what it was about. As far as I knew, my parents' insurance policy had paid for their burial expenses, and their estate—damn. Their estate. It hit me like a ton of bricks to the head. I hadn't thought about it during all the chaos.

I opened the envelope, and sure enough, it was a letter asking me to stop by for the reading of the will. I knew I was the sole heir. Shit. Shit. Shit. I hadn't been to Mom and Dad's at all since... Well, since it all happened. He wanted me to come by on Friday morning at eight a.m.

I handed it to Nicky, scrubbed my hand over my face, feeling the raised scar on my left cheek.

She looked over the papers for a minute. "Okay, do you want me to go with you?" Nicky asked, handing the paperwork back to me.

"Yes, of course. If you don't mind." I set the letter on the coffee table. "I can't believe I forgot about their estate, their house. I'm so...stupid. I think I've lost a few brain cells."

"Shut up, Char. No. You've been through hell, and you're allowed to forget shit." She stood to go to the kitchen and turned back to look at me. "Want some coffee?"

"Yeah. Thanks."

"And, by the way—who gives a fuck if you forget things? It happens."

Again, this was why I loved her. Always putting things in perspective, my kind of perspective, at least for the time being. She could be so crass, and I loved it.

***

Tonight was my first shift at The Styx, and I was nervous as hell. What had I been thinking? I was a damned detective; I didn't sling booze. When Nicky had said Wednesday's were slow, she was either lying, or this place was always slammed.

Standing behind the bar, I saw patrons lined up to the door and spread across the entire length of the place. Nicky was smiling and in her element. I was sweating like a pig just trying to figure out what kind of beer was

102

on tap. God forbid someone ordered a mixed drink. This had *not* been my best idea.

"Hey, black hair. Hey, you! I asked for a vodka on the rocks five minutes ago."

That guy was really getting on my nerves, and it had only been two minutes. I also had a name. He was about six feet tall with curly red hair and green eyes, looking like a linebacker.

I turned, smiling, sort of, and said, "My name is Charlotte, and your vodka on the rocks is sitting in front of you."

I grabbed my white bar towel and threw it over my shoulder. As I started to walk away, he grabbed my arm.

"You got a mouth on you, scar face. I don't want this fuckin' drink. Take it back."

I was done with his shit and looked him dead in the eye. "Get your fucking hand off me—*now*—before I remove it for you." Who did this asshole think he was?

"Or what?"

I picked up his glass and bashed him in the face—it shattered across his forehead. "This. Now get the fuck outta here, and never put your hands on another woman again, you piece of shit!"

He stumbled back, clutching his face *and* letting go of my arm. "You bitch!"

I put my hands on my hips and lifted a brow. "So I've been told. *Get out.*"

Johnny came running around the side of the bar, all six-feet-four of him. He was huge, with spiky dark-brown hair, brown eyes, and tatted sleeves on both giant, muscular arms— no one messed with him. Johnny yanked Red up by the collar and then dragged him out of The Styx.

"Char! What the hell happened? And on your first day?" Nicky was pissed, but not at me.

"The asshole put his hands on me, after I fixed his drink, then called me scar face, and said he no longer wanted his drink." I grabbed a glass and poured myself some water from the tap. "I warned him to take his hands off me, and he didn't listen, so I made him." I gulped down my water. I was fucking pissed.

"All right. Shit," Nicky said. "I can't believe this happened when I wasn't looking. I think you should go on home. I'm not mad at you, but I don't want anyone hurting you on accident. You can come back tomorrow night. I'll see you in a few hours." She took a deep breath, glancing around. "And next time, maybe try not to smash a glass in the customer's face. We could get sued, but as far as anyone here is concerned, no one saw a thing." She winked at me and patted me on the back.

"All right. No smashing of glasses—got it. If you're sure you don't need me for the rest of night." I was honestly ready to go home. This shit sucked. "I'll see ya in a while. I'm gonna shower and sleep."

Nicky hugged me and told me to be careful walking home. I untied my apron, hung it in the back, and left The Styx, ready for a hot shower. What the hell had I been thinking? Maybe tomorrow would be better? Or maybe I could help Johnny and be a bouncer—bash some heads together. That sounded good.

I left out of the back entrance around eleven thirty p.m. It was balmy outside, and I only had a couple blocks to walk, so I took my time. There were a few partygoers on the street, and several were falling-down drunk. I shook my head, thinking maybe I had made a bad decision.

Suddenly, my hackles rose, and it felt like someone was following me. Was it Big Red? I stopped, and swiftly turned to see who it was. But there was no one there. The alleyway was dark, though, and anyone could have been hiding in the shadows. My heart began racing in my chest, and I didn't have my gun. Shit.

I quickly cut through the alleyway to the main sidewalk onto St. Charles Boulevard. I could still feel someone's eyes on me. The sidewalk was a bit more crowded, and I felt safer. Surely, no one would attack me with witnesses hanging around. I *would* be carrying a weapon from now on. There was no way I was going through this shit again.

Quickening my pace, I headed straight for my apartment. I heard loud footsteps following behind me, and I'd had enough. I would *not* be afraid. Not anymore. I turned on my heel to face my would-be attacker.

"What the fuck do you—Greg! You asshole! Why are you following me like a stalker?"

He laughed and sidled up beside me. "I was just trying to catch up with you. Nicky told me what happened at the bar."

"Well, damn. All you had to do was say, 'Hey, Char! It's Greg,' not creep around behind me like a psycho. You were about to get the shit kicked outta ya."

"My bad. Care if I come up for a minute?"

I eyeballed him for a second. "I guess. But make it quick. I need a shower and my bed."

We made our way to my apartment; Greg was silent the entire walk up. I wondered what the hell was so important at near midnight. I unlocked the door and ushered him in after switching the light on.

Greg plopped down on my sofa, making himself at home.

"So, what's on your mind?" I sat in the chair next to the patio doors.

"It's about the case—"

I cut him off. "I don't wanna hear about this shit, Greg."

"I know, but you're the only one I can talk to about it. So, please, just listen for a minute." He gave me a pleading look, and I rolled my eyes.

I crossed my arms over my chest. "Fine. A few minutes."

"We think Francis might have an accomplice."

My heart stopped dead in my chest. "Why? What the hell makes you think that?"

"I didn't want to tell you, but there was another murder the other night, exactly the same calling card—everything fits. And Francis is behind bars. Either he has an accomplice, or we have a copycat killer on our hands. If we don't get a hold on it fast, they're talking about bringing in an FBI profiler."

"Fuck. This can't be happening." I was finally getting back to some semblance of normalcy, and now this?

"Char, you were the best detective we had on the Medley case. I know you don't want to come back, and you don't want to get involved, but we need your mind, your expertise on this one. If the FBI is brought in, Captain will have a shit fit, then it's out of our hands."

"My mind, Greg," I shouted, "my mind is fucked. Do you know I have nightmares of killing that bastard in different ways, several times a week?" I stood from my chair and paced the living room. "I can't stop the nightmares. I can't imagine getting involved with another serial killer case again."

"I'm sorry, Char. I am. I don't know what it's like to have lived through what you did, and I wouldn't ask—"

"But you are asking, Greg!" I stopped pacing and glared at him. "Look at what Francis did to me. Take a good look. Do you think I want to see more mutilated bodies and get into the mind of yet another serial killer attempting to pick up where he left off? It's only been four weeks."

"I know." Greg stood from the sofa and walked toward me. "Char, we need you. I hate what happened to you. I'm not asking you to come back, just be a consultant; help us put it together."

I put my head down. I didn't want another woman to die because I was too afraid of facing my own demons. I couldn't let that happen. But first, I'd have to exorcise those demons, and see the damn shrink.

"Listen, Davis wants me to see a shrink before I do anything. Let me talk to this person and get the go-ahead, then I'll see what I can do. I can't help you if I'm all messed up. Understand?"

Greg nodded and then wrapped his arms around me. "Thanks, Char. I really am sorry to have come to you like this, but you're the best. Whatever I can do to help you, I'm only a phone call away."

"I'm not promising anything, only that I'll try." I pulled away from him. "It'll be up to the shrink to decide. But I need you to do something for me: catch this killer if you can. We don't need another Medley running around."

Chapter 10

I watched in the shadow of night as Heather Finley met with her lover at Bayou St. John. She'd been running the trails alongside the eastern boundary of the New Orleans City Park. She'd been by no means discreet when she'd finished with him and sent him home to his wife.

Heather had been cautioned that her lewd behavior would end with deadly consequences, but she did not heed my warning. They never did.

Long red hair bounced behind her as she took each stride, her breasts taut in the tight sports shirt she was wearing. She had no idea what, or who awaited her. Just as she rounded the corner, I quickly stepped from behind the trees, and wrapped a thin ligature wire around her throat. Pulling her body flush to mine— leaving little room for struggle—I began dragging her into the darkened depths of the tall oak trees where no one could see or hear her.

Her breathing was shallow as I dragged her to the ground, still holding tight to the ligature. She was clawing at her neck, yet unable to utter even a syllable. The light in her hazel green eyes was beginning to fade, so I loosened my grip, tying it off behind her head. It wasn't her time to die yet. She needed to know why she had been chosen. And she needed to be able to respond to me.

I removed a steel blade from the tool belt I'd left near the tree and moved to straddle her waist. "Vanity, Heather." I slid my sharpened knife down the left side of her cheek, and she let out a raspy cry. The sound sent waves of pleasure skating over my skin, filling me with a sense of satisfaction and purpose, soothing me from the inside out. "Scream, little birdie. It's music to my ears."

I felt her cries strengthen my soul. I was the Harbinger of Death, the bringer of justice.

Heather's eyes grew wide with fear as blood streamed down her face. She tried desperately to swing at me with her hands, but it was in vain. What little breath she was able to draw was cut off as soon as she let go of the wire. It was almost time.

"You have been rendered untrustworthy. I am here to set you free."

I pulled tightly upon the ligature from behind her head, watching as the life drained from her soulless eyes. She never had a chance to fight back, just the way I had intended.

After slicing the front of her sports shirt with my knife, I slid the blade back into its rightful place, and then reached for my scalpel. Her pale, unmarred skin was on display now, and I felt my excitement rising within me. I held the scalpel tightly, unwilling to make a mistake. The incision had to be cut with precision, or it wouldn't be useful. Just above her uterus, where life was to be given, I proceeded to cut away my diamond strip of flesh.

Chapter 11

I had intended on going back to work at The Styx tonight, but after the conversation with Greg, I was a little unnerved. I wasn't exactly sure if I could get back into the game. I knew I needed to see a shrink, if only to rid myself of the horrendous nightmares, and deal with what Father Paul seemed to think was PTSD.

Although I had worked alongside others with PTSD in my profession, it wasn't something I wanted to accept. I had always been one to deal with my problems head-on, and I was afraid some psychiatrist would throw pills at me and call it good. That was not how I was going to handle this.

Nicky had arrived home in the early morning hours, after closing the bar, and I told her about the conversation with Greg. Needless to say, she was none too happy. She understood why I would want to help, but she agreed I needed to fix me first.

It was now ten a.m., and I felt like I'd barely slept a wink. I could hear Nicky stirring in the guest room and decided to get up and make some coffee. After setting the carafe to percolate, I grabbed my phone to call Captain Davis and set up a meeting with his damn psychiatrist. I realized if I didn't do it now, I would continue to put it off. I really didn't want to do this...

The phone rang three times before he answered.

"Captain Davis."

"Hey, Captain. It's Char—I mean, Detective Pierce. I've thought about what you said, and think I'll give your shrink a try."

I could hear him smiling through the phone. "I knew you would come around. I'm glad to hear it. I hope you're feeling better."

"This doesn't mean I'm coming back, just that I'll talk to someone like you suggested."

"All right, Charlotte. I'm just happy to hear you're getting out, and I think this will be good for you."

I sighed...heavily. "I hope you're right, Captain. Do you mind giving me his number?"

"Her number, yes. One moment."

I could hear him opening his drawer and moving things around. His desk was always a mess.

"Ah, here it is." He rattled off her number, and I wrote it down in a small green notepad lying on the table. "Georgia Henderson, but

Charlotte, she's not as bad as you think. At least give her a chance before you shut her down. I know how you can be."

"What's that supposed to mean?"

"You know exactly what I mean. It's no secret that you hold no love for psychiatry."

"Well, no. But..." He had me there. "Fine, we have a deal. I'll give her a shot."

"That's all I wanted to hear." He seemed awfully happy with himself.

I was scowling at the phone. "I better get going then. I'll give her a call and set up an appointment. Thanks, Captain."

"Anytime. Take care of yourself."

"Will do." I pushed the "END CALL" button and set the phone on the table.

Well, shit. I needed some coffee before I called this Georgia person.

Nicky walked into the dining room, looking rough, and scratching her head. "I smell coffee. You're the best."

She went to the kitchen and brought the carafe with two cups, then set everything on the table, sliding into her seat, yawning.

I poured myself a cup of coffee. "Thanks, Nicky. I was just about to get that. I was on the phone with the captain, and he gave me the number to his psychiatrist. Looks like I'm gettin' my head shrunk soon."

"Really? You're gonna go through with it? Well"—she sipped her coffee—"that's good. At least you're getting it over with. I mean, you need to talk to someone."

"I know, I just... well, if she can help, then okay." I took a drink of my coffee and then set it on the table. "Do you think I should call Jack and see if he can do the reading of the will today instead of tomorrow? I'd rather not wait."

"Char, honey, I've had two sips of coffee. I can't think just yet, but if that's what you want, all right."

Nicky's blonde hair was in a messy bun, sort of—basically sticking out all over her head—and it looked like she'd gone to bed without washing her face. She had mascara down to her cheekbones. So, I laughed at her "two sips of coffee" comment. Apparently, she didn't sleep well, either.

"I'll call him after I talk to the psychiatrist. If not, I can wait until Friday. I'm just feeling antsy. I kind of want to see Mom and Dad's things... Ya know?"

"Yeah, hon. I know." She set her mug down and touched my hand. "I'll help you go through everything if you want."

"Thank you. I appreciate that, Nicky."

Surprisingly, my heart didn't break when I thought of them. I was sad, and I missed them, but I was somewhat okay. Only time would tell once I walked into their house—smelled them. I prayed this time, that I would still be all right.

***

It was my lucky day. Georgia Henderson had an opening at one p.m. today and was more than happy to accommodate me. I tried to push it out until next week, but she was just *so* excited to "meet" me. I was *elated*. I couldn't believe I had actually agreed to this.

I climbed into my Chevy Tahoe, after placing my Glock 22 in my ankle holster, and headed toward the station. Yes, her office was actually located on the second floor of the building next door to the New Orleans Police Department. How convenient. I didn't want anyone to see me, so I decided I would use the back entrance and take the elevator. This was already turning out to be a bad idea. I wondered if this was Captain Davis's plan of setting me up to come back.

After sitting in traffic for what seemed like a year, I finally made it to the rear parking lot. The humidity slapped me in the face as soon as I opened the door to get out; it was unreal today and sweat was already pouring down my back. Eighties, my ass. It felt more like a hundred degrees. I couldn't get to that door fast enough. Well, to the AC, anyway. I honestly had no desire to speak to Georgia today, but it was best to get the intake exam over with.

I realized my fears were irrational, and I needed to suck it up and deal. Walking through the rear entrance, I pulled my curly black hair into a ponytail, kept my head down, and headed straight to stainless-steel elevators on my right. Pushing the "UP" button, I waited. And Waited.

Finally, I made it to the second floor and found her suite easily enough; it was room 210. It looked like any other doctor's office waiting room, with comfortable-looking chairs lining the walls, and a small TV suspended in the corner.

I went to the receptionist's window to check in. I was early. She knew who I was before I even told her my name. That was reassuring. After signing myself in, I took a seat against the back wall and picked up a magazine. No sooner than I opened it up, a woman looking to be in her mid- to late forties opened the side door, and asked me to come in.

Shit. My heart started pounding in my chest, but I stood anyway, and tried to smile. She was around five feet three inches tall, graying brown hair tied in a neat bun, and brown eyes, wearing khaki dress slacks and a white cardigan, with sensible neutral-colored heels.

Bland colors—to keep people from freaking out?

Opening the door wide, Georgia welcomed me in. "Hello, Charlotte. It's nice to meet you. Please, have a seat on the sofa."

Her office was nearly as bland as her clothing. The sofa was beige, resting against the far-left wall. Her mahogany desk sat in the corner to the left of the door, and there was a burgundy chair opposite the couch on the right, with a fully stocked bookshelf lining the wall behind it. A huge floor-to-ceiling window sat perched along the far wall, with fake plants decorating the floor. *Strange.*

I sat on the surprisingly comfortable sofa. "Thank you. Nice to meet you, too, Doctor Henderson."

"Please, call me Georgia," she said as she sat in the burgundy chair with her yellow legal pad clutched in her hands.

This was already extremely awkward, and I wanted to run outta there. I had no idea what to expect. *Hi, I'm Charlotte. Nice to meet you. See ya next week?* I could feel my nerves crawling around on the inside. This wasn't good.

I nodded. "Georgia it is, then." I didn't know what to do with my hands, so I folded them in my lap.

She leaned forward and fixed her brown eyes on me. "Just so you understand why you're here, and to help you feel more at ease, I am not going to make you relive the trauma you experienced, only help you deal with emotions associated with it, and find any underlying issues you may be having as a result.

"First, I'd like to get to know you. I understand it can be very difficult to speak to someone you've just met. Why don't we start with whatever makes you comfortable?" She leaned back into her chair and held her notepad in her lap, with a red pen in her right hand.

How was I supposed to answer that? Nothing about this situation made me comfortable. I didn't even want to be here. Maybe I should just tell her that.

I stopped fidgeting with my hands and decided honesty would be the best way to go. "Listen, this wasn't my first choice. I don't express myself very well, not when it comes to situations like this; it's all foreign territory for me. And to be honest, I'm terrified."

Georgia nodded, then scribbled something down on her notepad. "What exactly are you afraid of?"

"Nightmares. I keep having them. Panic attacks when I talk about what happened to me, or how he killed my parents." I closed my eyes and took a deep breath. "I know you're aware of what happened with Francis Medley, so there's no need for me to go into detail, and I don't want to. I just want the nightmares to stop."

I couldn't believe I'd just blurted all that out. This was not what I had planned. In fact, I thought I would only be doing a meet-and-greet today. I guessed everyone was right, and I really did need to talk to someone who didn't know me.

"I can understand that," Georgia said. "How would you feel about answering a short questionnaire? It will help me determine your mindset at present, and what you're feeling on a day-to-day basis. This is typically standard procedure for an intake exam such as yours." She pulled a sheet of paper from a white binder sitting on the table next to her. "If at any time you feel yourself becoming agitated, or unable to answer the question, just skip the question and move on to the next. Do you think you're up for that?"

I nodded, not really feeling it, but knew it was necessary if I wanted to get through this. Attaching the questionnaire to a clipboard, she handed it to me.

When I observed the questionnaire, my heart stopped in my chest. They were questions concerning problems people sometimes have in response to a "stressful experience." I was to read each one and circle a number to indicate how much I had been "bothered" by said problem within the last two weeks.

The first one: Repeated, disturbing, and unwanted memories of the stressful experience. *Seriously?*

Second: Disturbing dreams of the stressful experience. *Oh, my God.*

Third: Suddenly feeling or acting as if the stressful experience were happening again (as if you were actually back there, reliving it).

I continued on down the list: blaming myself, super alert or on guard, difficulty concentrating or falling asleep, strong feelings of fear, horror, or anger, aggressive behavior... I had to stop. Nearly everything applied to me in an extreme way. I wondered what the hell this meant, and if by answering these questions, what would Georgia glean from my psyche? Was I crazy?

I held back my tears and answered the questions as best I could, circling the numbers as required. By the time I was finished, my hands were trembling. I wasn't sure if I could go through with this. I never wanted to see that damn sheet of paper again. It reminded me of everything that I was trying to avoid.

I handed the clipboard back to Georgia and waited, wringing my hands together, staring at the ceiling. I wondered if my allotted hour was up yet.

Once Georgia was finished reviewing my answers, she set the clipboard onto the table next to her chair. "Charlotte, based on the answers you've given, and my professional opinion, it seems you're experiencing symptoms of Post-Traumatic Stress Disorder, which is not uncommon for someone who has been through what you have, and lived."

There it was again—that diagnosis—the one I feared, but in my gut, knew to be true. I only nodded in response. I didn't have much to say and let her continue.

"I realize this is our first session together, and you're probably wondering what a preliminary diagnosis like this means." She set her pen on the table, clasping her hands in her lap. "People live with PTSD every day. While it is not easy, once you learn your triggers, and ways to cope with the emotions associated with them, it is possible to live a somewhat normal life—a new normal, if you will. You just have to put in the work.

"I believe the first thing, as you said, is dealing with the cause of your nightmares. This is one of the most common elements after a traumatic experience, and one that may continue for quite some time. However, there are several ways to relax your mind, and learn of things in your daily routine that might be setting them off."

I had to stop her there. "Well, it's only been a little over four weeks. I'd say everything in my life sets them off."

"Quite true. You need time to readjust into your life. I've found journaling helps: letting out your feelings on paper, writing letters you will never send, and releasing your pain when you feel it welling up inside. These are things you have control over. You, retaking control of your life; that's what is most important.

"Control is a huge factor here. When you feel you are in control, it will become easier for you to notice your triggers, and then deal with them as they come. That is what I want to help you with: coping, and then living again."

What she was saying sounded wonderful—but getting there. I knew I had a long way to go before I could regain *all* of my control, but to me, it was worth it. I was not going to allow that psychotic shitbag to control me, or every aspect of my life. And this was my first step.

I stood from the sofa. "Thank you, Georgia. I'm not sure if our time is up, but I want you to know that you've helped me to understand a few things. You're not as bad as I thought you'd be." I leaned over, smiling, and shook her hand.

She smiled back and then stood. "I'm happy to help. I'd like to see you at least once a week, if possible. The quicker we get a handle on this, the easier life will become. Next session, you can do some talking, and we can get on with your treatment." She patted my arm and then led me to the door. "Next Wednesday at two should work, if that's all right with you."

"Yes, Wednesday is fine. I'll see you then." I walked out of her office and through the door to the hallway, feeling much better. I now had a plan. A plan to help myself get through the mess that was my mind—and regaining control of my life once again.

Chapter 12

God, the heat. When I climbed back into my Tahoe, it was like a furnace. I turned the AC on full blast and waited. I hated New Orleans summers, the humidity, anyway. My cell started ringing, and I had to dig into my bag to find it. Greg's face lit up my screen. Shit. I wondered what he wanted now, and I hoped it wasn't about the case. I wasn't ready yet.

I answered the call. "Hey, Greg. What's up?"

"Hey, Char. I hope I didn't call at a bad time. Do you have a minute?"

"Yeah, I'm just melting in the heat right now. Don't be surprised if you find a puddle of me next door to the station. It's freakin' hot." I fanned myself, waiting for the AC to kick in.

He laughed. "A puddle? Should I even ask?"

"Well, I had my first session with the department's psychiatrist today. Did you know her office is right next door? I kinda feel like this was a set-up."

Damn, it was so hot! Sweat was pouring down my face and into my tank top. Gross.

"No, I didn't, but since you're close, do you mind coming by the station? I have some news, and no it's not about the copycat case, but something I think you should be aware of."

Was he out of his mind? "Greg, that's honestly the last place I want to be right now. Why?"

"Listen, this isn't something I want to tell you over the phone, so why don't I meet you in the parking lot, and we can take the back way into the captain's office."

The captain's office? What the hell could this be about? I was not going to be forced to come back. No. If that's what they wanted, then they, along with the entire station would hear my thoughts on the matter.

"Fine. Meet me in the rear parking lot next door. You can't miss my white Tahoe. I'll just sit here and try not to fry until you find me."

"All right. See ya in a few."

He ended the call, and I looked in the backseat for the light green jacket I'd brought with me. The last thing I wanted was for everyone to stare at my scars. I didn't want their damn pity.

I scrolled through my phone, seeing a missed call from Jack Flanigan. Damn. I didn't

128

have time to call him back. I listened to the voicemail instead. He said he was completely booked today but could see me as early as eight a.m. tomorrow morning. The same time we already had scheduled. So, seeing him today was a wash.

A loud knock on my window caused me to throw my phone into the floorboard. "What the fuck, Greg?" I opened the door. "Can you stop sneaking up on me?" I leaned down to pick up my cell and stuffed it inside my pants pocket.

"Sorry, Char. I didn't mean to. I just knocked." He shrugged, with his hands in his pockets. He looked like he hadn't been sleeping much, with black circles resting beneath his eyes.

I guessed I was a little jumpy, but he could have called. My heart was still beating frantically when I closed and locked the door to my vehicle.

"It's fine. I'm just a little off, that's all. Any way you can tell me what this is all about without having to go inside the station?"

"No, not really. The captain wants to talk to you, too."

Great.

"Fine, but if this is some ploy to—"

"Stop, Char. It's not. It'll be fine."

We walked into the back entrance of the station, and my heart wouldn't stop trying to remove itself from my chest. I did *not* want to be here.

We took the stairs up to the captain's office, and Greg walked right in. I'd seen a few uniformed officers on the way up, but thankfully none of them paid attention to me.

The captain's office was a mess, with filing cabinets hanging open, stacks of casefiles on his desk, and even the picture hanging on the wall behind his desk sat askew. It looked like he had been sleeping in here; there were blankets and a pillow lying on the black leather couch against the wall near the door.

Closing the door behind me, I greeted him, "Hey, Captain. Greg tells me there's information I need to know. What's going on?" I sat in the chair opposite his desk and let out a heavy breath. Greg stood next to the captain.

"Thank you for coming," Captain Davis said, pushing a casefile away, then clasping his hands in front of him. "I know this isn't easy, you being here, but we need you to know what's going on with Medley."

"What the hell, Greg?" I glared at him. "I thought this wasn't about the case."

Greg stepped forward and took the seat next to me. "It's not, Char. It's about Medley, not the copycat, or whatever. Please, just listen to what happened, and then make your own decision."

I sat back in the chair and folded my arms against my chest. "Go on. What happened? Did someone kill him in lock-up?" I hoped so.

"No, but Greg—Detective Stevenson—went in to question Francis about the latest murder and attempted to pry a few details from him about an accomplice. The son of a bitch acted like he was insane."

"He *is* insane," I said. "What makes this any different?"

"It's what he said, and how he was acting that gave us all pause." Davis cleared his throat. "He ignored our questions about an accomplice, and spoke in riddles, smiling the entire time. He would only talk about you."

There it was. Why they wanted me here, and what the hell?

"That's just too damned bad. I'm a witness, the only *living* witness to his sadistic crimes, and he doesn't get to talk to me." I was

131

shaking from the inside out. What did the piece of shit want from me?

"Yes, Charlotte, we know this." The captain ran his hands through his hair. "The thing is, he lawyered up, and said he will only speak to you. He wanted to know how you were doing, talking about things I'd rather not discuss. Detective Stevenson had to be restrained from kicking his ass. The bastard just laughed, saying your name, over and over."

I leaned forward in my chair and leveled my eyes on Captain Davis. "Okay, so he's batshit. Why are you telling me this?"

"It's not what he said, but the implications behind it. We believe, if he does have an accomplice, or even a copycat fulfilling his *work*, your life might be in danger once again."

Greg was silent, but I could hear him breathing. My hands became sweaty, and I felt like I was going to have a heart attack. I stood from my chair and began pacing within the small confines of the office. The blinds were open, and I could see a few detectives loitering near the door, so I slammed them shut.

I was in control. Francis was behind bars; he couldn't hurt me. I'd kill any son of a bitch who tried to harm me again. I stopped and turned, looking between the two of them.

"So, what do you want me to do, hide inside my apartment? I'm not going to do that. I'm not cowering in fear because of some crazed lunatic's ramblings."

Greg looked up at me. "That's not what we're saying at all. But the captain and I discussed maybe having a patrol officer watching your building."

"Are you fucking kidding me?"

I was not going to have my privacy invaded by someone who didn't know me, or even what to look for. Drunkards walked up and down my street all the time. And what of the nights I worked at the bar? Would this officer be in there, too, watching my every move? Hell no. I was *not* having that.

I could hear Captain Davis sigh. "I know this isn't what you want. Hell, none of us would, but after what happened, I don't want your safety jeopardized. Will you at least think about it?"

I knew that maybe I was being unreasonable, but I wanted my life back, and I didn't want someone breathing down my neck every time I turned around.

"Look, I'll think about it, all right? But right now, I'm trying to fix me, find some sense of normalcy again. I can't have that if I feel

133

someone watching me all the time." I sat down in my chair and wiped my sweaty hands on my pants. "I'll make you a deal: if things get worse, and I start to feel unsafe, I'll let you put a patrol on me. It's the best I can do."

Captain Davis nodded. "All right then. Just keep us informed, and if you suspect anything at all, I need you to call someone right away. Don't try to handle this on your own."

Greg's phone rang, and he answered. I could only hear part of the conversation, but by his cursing, it didn't sound good.

"Captain, we've got another body. This one's over by the New Orleans City Park. I'll call you as soon as I know something." He looked at me. "Char, I've gotta run. I'll talk to you soon."

Fuck. I hoped it wasn't another copycat murder. None of this set well with me. The fact that Francis was asking for me, and saying God only knows what? I was attempting to keep my composure, but inside, I was afraid they could be right.

"Okay, Captain. You guys have a lot going on. I'm gonna head out. I'll be in touch." I stood and then shook his hand.

"Charlotte, please be safe, and take care of yourself."

"Will do, Captain."

With that, I opened the door and closed it behind me. Stephanie Hamilton was standing just outside when I turned around. I nearly smacked right into her.

"Hey, Charlotte. Sorry about that," she said. "I'm glad you're here. I wanted to apologize about what happened a couple weeks ago. I didn't know... I just... I'm sorry." She hung her head, twisting her hands together.

Now I really felt like shit. "Stephanie, it's fine. I was in a bad place, and it's not your fault. I was rude and shouldn't have been. If anything, I should apologize to you."

"Thank you, but that's not necessary." She looked down the hallway. "Did Greg say where he was going? I just tried to call his cell, but he didn't answer."

"Yeah, he said another body was found near New Orleans City Park. Why didn't you go with him?"

I could see the fury burning in her eyes. "Son of a bitch! This is the second time he's done this to me. I'm supposed to be his partner, but he leaves me out of everything—never taking my calls, and barely discussing the case with me."

"Why the hell would he do that?" I asked as she walked with me down the hall toward the stairwell. "It's not like him."

"Hell, if I know. But I'm putting a stop to this shit today. I'm done being treated like I don't know how to do my job."

I paused at the door and looked into her eyes. "Stephanie, do not allow *anyone* to stop you from doing your job. If you have to take over and be a bitch while doing so, then do it. People don't have to like it, but they *will* respect you for it."

"Thanks, Charlotte, because that's exactly what I'm about to do. I've had enough. I'll talk to you later. I'm heading out to the scene, and Greg can kiss my ass."

I nudged her shoulder and grinned. "Good girl. Kick him in the balls for me."

"I might. Don't tempt me." She walked past me to other end of the hallway, and I took the stairs to the parking lot.

What the hell was Greg thinking? I had to wonder. Why wouldn't he want Stephanie involved in the case? It didn't make any sense.

Chapter 13

On the way home, the captain's words kept playing over and over in my mind. I wondered what kind of twisted game Francis was playing, and why he wanted to talk to me. I could feel the panic rising in my chest at the thought of seeing him, but I pushed it back down. There was no point in dwelling over something that wasn't going to happen, at least not until the trial.

What had he said that had gotten Greg so worked up, though? I wasn't about to ask. I would only be putting my mind in even more turmoil than it already was. I kept trying to shake the unease I felt in my gut. I was going to be okay, and I would not allow Francis to get inside my head again. I was in control. I had to be.

Once I pulled into the parking lot of my apartment, I decided I would go ahead and work tonight at The Styx. If I wanted to be normal, then I needed to do normal things, like work, and not sit around watching mindless TV.

When I opened the door, Nicky was sitting on the couch. "How did it go with the shrink?"

"Pretty well, actually." I set my bag and keys on the table near the door. "A lot better than I expected. I have another appointment scheduled for next Wednesday at two."

I was still trembling inside, and knew I needed to calm my racing thoughts. I wished the captain wouldn't have told me what Francis had said. I understood why he and Greg were worried for my safety, but the news wasn't helping my current mindset. And then, another murder...

"Charlotte, hon, you're shaking. What's going on?" Nicky's voice broke me from my thoughts. I hadn't realized my emotions were showing on the outside.

"I had to go to the station." I pulled my hair from its ponytail and sat on the couch next to her. "Greg called after my appointment, saying he had information I needed to hear. Both he *and* the captain wanted to talk to me."

"About what? I thought you told them you wanted nothing to do with the case. Why do they insist on involving you? Damn them!" Nicky slammed her fists on the couch.

"I know, but it wasn't about the latest case. They talked with Medley, and he had a few things to say, and not about an accomplice. He only wanted to talk to me, and asked how I was doing—"

She cut me off. "Why the fuck would they tell you something like that?"

"Well, mostly because he was acting more insane than usual, and some of the things he did say, which they didn't tell me, caused them to worry about my safety. They think it's possible my life might be in danger and wanted to station a patrol officer outside. I told them no."

Nicky's eyes went wide. "Why did you say no? Char, if your life is in danger, then it would be safe to say, having a cop nearby is a good thing."

"Because, it's not. I don't want someone breathing down my neck twenty-four-seven, especially with me working at the bar. No." I threw my head back on the couch. "Nicky, I'm trying to find normal, and having someone watching me is *not* normal."

"But, Char, you're not thinking about this rationally, and before you punch me, just listen. If there's another killer out there who wants you dead, and possibly working with Francis, you need to have every safety measure in place."

"I have my gun. And I'm not about to act like a dumbass again and take on a killer on my own. I'm never alone, and that's why working at the bar is such a good idea. See? Normal."

"No, I don't see." She huffed out a sigh. "Are you at least gonna think about it?"

"Yeah, that's exactly what I told them. If I feel it necessary, then I'll let them know. Until then, I just want to be left the hell alone."

"Fine, but I think you're making a bad call here. I know how much you enjoy your privacy, hell, I do too, but I want you to be safe. That's all."

"I know, Nicky, and I'll be careful. I'm just not going to live in fear—I can't, not if I want some kind of peace in my life." I stood from the couch. "I'm gonna take a nap before my shift tonight. I promise I won't smash anyone in the face this time." I grinned and then walked toward my room.

She laughed at me. "All right, I'll wake you up in a few hours with some coffee."

I was so exhausted after not sleeping well, and then after everything today, I just wanted to sleep. I stripped down and crawled into my bed, setting my gun on the bedside table.

***

Someone was calling my name—a familiar voice—Francis! I was running through a large, open concrete tunnel with my gun at my side. Where the hell was I? I could hear his voice, singing my name, like some kind of cadence; it echoed off of the concrete walls.

I continued running toward the sound of his voice, my heart beating like a drum in my chest. He wanted to see me? Fine. He would meet the barrel of my gun. I was ending this once and for all.

Shadows danced along the walls as I ran, and an eerie chill raced down my spine. His voice seemed closer now, but I couldn't see him. Where the hell was he? I stopped, my gun at the ready, searching the dimly lit tunnel for a door or a place where he could be hiding. I walked slowly, remaining aware of my surroundings, still hearing his menacing echo all around me.

"Come on out, Francis. I'm here. Isn't that what you want? Face me, you coward!"

"Little birdie, little birdie—come out and play. Charlotte, sweet Charlotte—what do you say?" Francis was singing in riddles, and now, this? Psycho.

I crept closer, keeping to the left side of the tunnel. The light from the sun was at my back, but I knew he was close.

"Fuck you!"

"Little birdie, little birdie—let's play a game. Charlotte, sweet Charlotte—what is your real name?"

What the—? My real name? I'd always been Charlotte, except my last name had been Hernandez before I was adopted. Screw this shit. I wasn't listening to this anymore. I took off running again, and then I saw him—and I stopped.

Francis stepped from an alcove on my right, licking a steel blade, a malicious gleam in his eyes. "Let's play a game, little birdie." He took two steps toward me and held the knife in front of him, nearing my face. I didn't move. "This is my game, after all—"

"I'm not playing your fucking game." I fired off a shot, hitting him between the eyes. "Game over, bitch." Then I shot him again in his groin.

He was dead.

I turned on my heel and began running toward the light at the end of the tunnel.

***

I awoke with a start, sweat dripping down my face. Not again. Another nightmare, but not in his basement this time. I sat up in bed and thought about what Georgia had said. My waking moments, things that happened throughout the day could affect my dreams. *Thanks, Greg.* If I hadn't agreed to talk to him and the captain, then I wouldn't have just shot Francis in the face in my dream.

I shuddered as gruesome images from my nightmare flashed before my eyes. Why did I keep dreaming of killing him? Was it something in my mind, attempting to fight back in my sleep, because I hadn't been able to when he'd attacked me? I had no idea, but it was freaking me the hell out.

It was no secret, if he accidentally hung himself in prison, or someone shanked him, I wouldn't shed a tear. But seeing myself killing him over and over again while I slept was something else altogether. I couldn't shake it, or the overwhelming panic that took up space in my mind afterward. It was all just too much.

I needed to write it all down like Georgia had recommended. Hell, it couldn't hurt. Maybe then, I could pour these emotions out on paper, and not into another damned nightmare. I'd start on it tonight after work and pray for a peaceful night's sleep.

I threw my covers back and went to take a shower. I had to be at work in less than two hours anyway.

"Char?" I heard Nicky call out from my room. "You all right? I heard you tossing and turning, but I didn't want to wake you. Made you some coffee, though."

"Just another nightmare. I'll tell you about it after I'm dressed. Be out in a few."

Just another nightmare where I'd shot Francis dead. A cold shiver traversed my entire body at the thought. I hoped Georgia could help me find a way to stop these horrific dreams.

"Okay, I'm gonna fix us a bite to eat before our shift starts."

"Thanks!" If she didn't stop feeding me, my ass was gonna be as large as the broad side of a barn.

I finished my shower and decided a messy bun would do tonight. Curly hair was just gonna frizz anyway. There was no point in fixing it in this humidity. I threw on a pair of black stretchy pants, white tank and mid-length, quarter-length sleeved black jacket with black shit-kicking boots for work. Also strapping my Glock 22 to my ankle; there was no way I would be leaving home without it again.

When I walked into the dining room, Nicky let out a low whistle. "Don't you look snazzy?"

"Snazzy?" I laughed at the expression on her face. "Really? Who says that?"

"I do, smart ass. Here's your coffee." She handed me a cup, and I took a sip—just what I needed. "I was just sayin', you look nice. I like the little coat."

"Oh, thanks. I've had it forever. It covers a lot of my scars, but soon enough, the nasty red-looking ones will fade, and I won't care anymore."

"Scars, or not, you're beautiful the way you are."

I slid into my seat at the table. "Thanks, I just don't want people staring and then asking questions I'm not prepared to answer."

"Well, for one, if anyone were to ask, you could just tell them to fuck off; it's none of their business. That's just rude." She set her mug down and looked at me with a serious expression. "And two, you have no reason to hide those scars if you don't want to. They're battle scars, and you lived. Screw everyone else."

I knew she was right, but it was more than people questioning my scars; I just wasn't ready to put them on display. I was still healing, and not just on the outside. These dreams were tearing me apart more than I'd let on. I felt like I was reliving everything all over again, even though each one ended in his death.

"I know you're right. I'm sure I'll get past it eventually, but for now, I just want to be comfortable in my own skin without the thought of people staring. I have enough goin' on in my head as it is."

"Speaking of your head, you said you had another nightmare?" She grabbed a muffin from the bowl on the table and took a bite.

"Yeah, no basement this time. It was freakin' creepy as hell. I was in some kinda concrete tunnel, and he was singing these strange riddles. When he stepped out with his knife, I shot him in the face and then his balls. That about sums it up."

Nicky's mouth fell open. "What the—? Oh, my God. Well, that was... different. Shit. A bit disturbing."

"I know. My psychiatrist said I need to start writing things down and mentioned that what happens in my day-to-day life can affect my dreams. Pretty sure that's why I had this particular nightmare—the meeting at the station."

"This is exactly why I wish they would just let you be and allow you to heal. Damn, Char.

It hasn't even been six weeks. Don't they know shit like that can mess with you?" She leaned back in her chair and crossed her arms. "I can see Greg being a selfish prick. But your captain; I'd like to think at least he would take a little more caution."

"I was thinking the same, but the captain's thinking about my safety. Greg, well, who the hell knows?" I shrugged. "He's acting strange these days. I think he's under a lot of pressure because of the threat of an FBI profiler coming in."

"Well, he's an ass. Grab your sandwich so we can get ready to go. I told Johnny I'd come in a little early to help stock the bar."

"Yes, ma'am." I grabbed my sandwich to go and headed for the door. I hoped we wouldn't have another incident in the bar.

Chapter 14

Thursday nights were packed; the crowd was larger than it had been yesterday. I was thankful that Nicky had taken the time to show me how to make a few drinks after helping Johnny stock the bar. Another bartender, named Jessica, was working tonight, too.

"Hey, Char, wanna help me with this order?" Jessica yelled from the other end of the bar. "We have two for Sex on the Beach, and one Lemon Drop Martini. I can show you how to mix them."

"Sure, just one sec." I set a Corona in front of a tall, dark-haired man. "That'll be four dollars." He gave me a five-dollar bill and told me to keep the change.

Turning toward Jessica, I noticed she had her hands full. Men and women were yelling their orders over each other at her end of the bar. Jessica's pink-and-blonde hair was tied up in a ponytail, showcasing a swirling tribal tattoo beginning from her neck, looking like it went all the way down her back.

Jessica was dressed in a black tank and black pants. She had a diamond-stud piercing in the right side of her nose, a silver ring in her lip, and a few piercings up the side of each ear. She looked to be in her mid- to late twenties. I had no idea. I'd only met her a few times.

"Hey, what can I do to help?" I grabbed three beers she was holding, and she pointed to who they belonged to. I lined them up in front of the men who'd ordered them, they paid for their drinks, and three more patrons took their place.

"I've already made the Sex on the Beach. I'll show you the Lemon Drop Martini real quick. It's super easy." She pointed to a list above the register. "If you ever get lost, here's a list of ingredients for each drink. It's a real life saver."

"Thanks, Jessica." I watched as she made the drink, taking note of all the components. "Here, let me handle it—you've got enough going on down there. Who does it need to go to?" She nodded toward a young blonde woman, who seemed to be arguing with her boyfriend. Shit.

I set the drink in front of her, and before I could tell her how much she owed, her drunk-looking, blonde-haired boyfriend interrupted me. "She's done. She's not drinking that shit." His brown eyes were cold and unmoving. I wondered what this poor woman had to deal with on a daily basis.

I eyed the drink and then looked at her. She had a pleading look on her face. What was with some men, believing they had the right to tell any woman what to do, boyfriend or not?

"Ma'am, do you still want your drink?" I looked directly into her blue eyes, ignoring the assbag standing beside her.

"You heard what I said, bitch. She doesn't want it!" Then I saw his hand firmly gripping her arm.

"Sir, I'm going to have to ask you to leave." I looked to the blonde woman. "You can stay if you want." I glanced at her arm, making sure she knew I could see his hands on her.

"Who the hell do you think you are? She's coming with me." He jerked her off the barstool, and she went tumbling to the floor. My blood started boiling.

"Johnny!" I called out, before this became a problem. I was ready to smash the asshole's face into the bar, but I figured it wouldn't be a good idea after what happened last night.

In an instant, Johnny was on the blonde prick, and told him it was time to go. The guy must have been drunk; he took a swing, and Johnny laid him out onto the floor. I was already around the other side of the bar, helping his girlfriend to her feet. She was crying. Where the hell was Nicky?

Johnny dragged his sorry ass out, and I led his girlfriend to a corner table. "Hey, my name's Charlotte. You all right? Can I get you anything?" I felt so bad for her.

"Thank you, no. I think I just need a cab. Derrick is always like this when he drinks, but he's really a nice guy." She dried her tears with a napkin from the dispenser on the table. I'd heard these stories a million times. They were always nice, until they were drunk and beating you.

"I can call you a cab, but are you sure you're gonna be all right?" I sat beside her in the chair to her right. "Look, I realize it's not my place to butt in, but I can't help it. I used to be a cop, and I'm not trying to scare you, only help you. If he hits you now, who's to say he won't hit you again?"

She nodded, tears still flowing down her face. "He's only hit me once. I can handle it."

I handed her another napkin to dry her still-falling tears. "All right, but if you ever need anything, please don't hesitate to call someone. I'll go get you that cab. Just sit tight."

I stood and walked away from her. I wanted to help her, but I knew there was no way I could help someone who wasn't ready to help herself. It made my heart hurt. No one should ever have to suffer abuse from anyone.

After calling her a cab, I went back to the bar and served several more customers, before I finally saw Nicky. She looked a little upset.

"Nic, what's wrong?" I turned to her and walked toward the back.

She rubbed her forehead nervously. "My brother, Randy, was in an accident. He's okay, just a broken collarbone, a few bumps and bruises. They're keeping him overnight because he has a concussion. The doctor's want to make sure there's no swelling on his brain."

"Oh, my God! When did this happen?" I hugged her and then pulled away. "Are you going to be okay to drive? Do you need me to take you to the hospital?"

"About an hour ago, and no, it's fine. I'm just gonna run by his house and get him some clothes, toiletries and things. I'll probably stay the night. Do you think you can close up with Jessica and Johnny?"

"Of course! Whatever you need, just call me and let me know how he's doing. Please be careful, and text me when you get to the hospital." I hugged her again.

Nicky rarely showed emotion, but her parents were dead, too. She only had her little brother. I could tell she was pretty shaken up, and rightfully so.

"I will, Char. And if you need anything, call me, all right?"

"I'll be fine. You just take care of you and your brother. Love ya lots."

"Love ya back." She turned away from me before I could see her cry. I hoped Randy would be okay. If not, Nicky would lose her shit.

I walked back to the bar, and it looked like Johnny was cleaning house. I'd heard a scuffle going on in the background but didn't realize what had happened until now. Apparently, another drunk didn't like the way Johnny had handled the situation with blondie's boyfriend and thought to tell him as much.

I had an internal facepalm going on. I wondered if fighting was a nightly occurrence around here. Damn. He had three men, throwing them out, and others were yelling, cursing and throwing shit.

I'd had it. I was not going to work under these conditions. I climbed up on the bar and stood. "That's enough!" I shouted at the top of my lungs, eyeing the crowd. "Throw something, hit someone, or even look at anyone like you're gonna start a fight, and you're outta here!"

Well, that got their attention. The entire bar stopped what they were doing and looked at me, even Johnny, who was grinning from ear to ear. I climbed down from the bar, and yelled, "Who's next? I don't have all night."

I wasn't exactly made for customer service, I decided, but enough was enough. This was bullshit. However, I did make a statement, and the bar calmed the fuck down.

Jessica came over and slapped me on the back. "Now that was some good shit. Funny, but effective. Good one."

"Thanks." I wasn't going for funny, but whatever worked.

Finally, after about an hour, people were clearing out, and I only had two orders left. I was pouring a beer on tap when I felt someone behind me.

A hand on my shoulder sent beer flying all over the floor. I quickly turned to see Greg's face. "What the hell? You're not supposed to be back here. Get your ass on the other side of the bar, and stop sneaking up on me, jackass!"

"Sorry, I heard about your little 'standing on the bar' show, and thought I'd rib you about it."

"Have you been here all this time?" What was his problem, and why was he acting like this?

"I have something you need to see. Maybe we should take a table in the back."

"I swear to— Greg, you've done enough today, and you're not exactly my favorite person right now. What do you want?"

"Sorry I scared you. It's important, though. Come on, it'll only take a few minutes."

I stared at him, wondering what was going on inside his head, and what it was that was so important, he had to come all the way to the bar to show me.

"Jess, I'll be back in a few minutes." She nodded that she heard me and went back to work. Folding my arms, I looked at Greg. "This better be good, or I'm banning you from the bar."

"You wouldn't." He laughed as he walked toward the table in the back.

I most certainly would if he didn't straighten his ass up. I was tired of his stupid games.

I sat down at the table and placed my hands in front of me. "What is it? And make it quick; I'm working."

He sighed and then pulled a casefile from his jacket. Fuck. "This, and before you storm off, there's a reason I'm giving you this information."

I sat back in my chair and raised a brow. "Is it about the murder in New Orleans City Park this morning?"

"Yes, but there's more. It also solidifies what the captain and I were telling you this morning. Take a look." He slid the file across the table, placing it in front of me.

I took a deep breath, not wanting to open that damned casefile, but I did it anyway. The first thing I saw was a picture of Heather Finley's face, and my heart fell to the floor. I'd grown up with Heather. We went to high school together, but I hadn't talked to her in a few years.

Then I saw her body—staged—just like the Medley killings. The same diamond-shaped calling card, deep cut on her left cheek, and oh, my God, she'd been strangled, too. All the

156

same. I absently rubbed the scar on my cheek and felt myself falling into memories of my past. Was this killer now targeting people close to me, people I knew? Oh, God. I thought of Nicky.

I felt panic rising in my chest; my breathing became shallow, and I clutched my neck. "Char! Are you all right? Talk to me," Greg said, placing his hands on my shoulders.

"No." I couldn't say much else, seeing Heather's mutilated body. I knew her mother, her sisters, and God, her kids. She had twin boys. "I can't do this, Greg." I shoved the casefile back at him, attempting to rein in the panic that threatened to take over my mind and body.

"I'm sorry. I just thought you would want to know. This is too damn close, and you need to stay on alert; be aware of your surroundings." He removed his hands from my shoulders and looked into my eyes. "I know this is hard, but you're my partner, and I need you."

I snapped. This was not happening. "No, *Greg*. Stephanie is your partner, and you need to treat her as such. I am *still* on medical leave, and I'm not sure if I'm ever coming back." I balled my fists together to keep from hitting him. "You need to get that through your thick skull. I've been to one therapy session. *One.* Did you *not* hear what I said when I told you I couldn't make any promises?"

He sat back in his chair with an angry expression. "You need to just get over this shit and do your job."

"What the fuck did you just say to me?" I near shouted, standing from my chair. "Get over it? Have you lost your damn mind? Can I not have time to heal and deal with what happened to me? It happened to *me*"—I banged my fist against my chest—"not you. Me! Get the fuck outta here. Now." I pointed toward the door, and I saw Johnny come running my way.

"Is there a problem here, Char?" Johnny eyed Greg like he wanted to beat him to a bloody pulp.

Greg stood, picking up the casefile. "No, I was just leaving. Have a nice night, *Charlotte.*"

My full name? In all the time I'd known him, Greg had always only called me Char. Well, he could just fuck all the way off. He could stay pissed. I had zero shits to give.

158

Chapter 15

I watched from the darkened shadows as Charlotte and Jessica cleaned the bar; they'd told Johnny to go home for the night. She had no idea I was watching her every move, listening to every word she spoke. Charlotte had a lesson to learn, one she hadn't learned the first time.

The women had decided to throw back shots of tequila after closing the bar and dimming the lights. Charlotte's face, although scarred, was still beautiful, but she needed to know what happened when she defied the Harbinger of Death.

I waited patiently, observing, biding my time. Shot after shot consumed, I listened to incessant laughter as it grated against my nerves. Charlotte had never been one who could hold her liquor, and it didn't take long before her head began to nod forward.

Jessica continued nudging her, insisting she drink one more shot, and Charlotte fell for the woman's tricks each time. This Jessica, she had a story, one that only few people knew of. But I did. I always knew.

Again, I waited.

Charlotte propped her head on the bar, and I could hear her soft snoring. She had passed out from the tequila. I could see Jessica grabbing something from her purse, and then she headed toward the ladies' room, leaving Charlotte all alone.

When the bathroom door closed, I ensured Charlotte was out cold. Keeping to the shadows, I slowly opened the door just enough to where I could go in unnoticed.

Jessica was snorting a line of coke from the counter. Silently, I pulled the ligature wire from my jacket and stepped behind her, wrapping it tightly around her neck. She jerked, surprised, but unable to remove the wire, and clumsily pulled at her throat.

I yanked harder, dragging her to the filthy floor. She kicked her legs wildly, but to no avail. I sat on her stomach; her breathing was shallow now.

Her bloodshot blue eyes were wide with fear—I wanted her to fear me. Holding the ligature with my right hand, I reached for the scalpel in my coat pocket with the other. Tonight would be different. She had to pay for Charlotte's inability to heed the warnings she'd been given.

With my left hand, I made a deep laceration down the left side of her face, ensuring to hold

160

onto the ligature, so no sound could escape her filthy mouth. It was open in a silent scream, and although her cries would have given me pleasure, removing her tongue would fill me with excitement, knowing Charlotte would find her dead body.

Strangling Jessica until death met what used to be her drug-induced stare, I released the wire, then pried her mouth open, cutting out her tongue and placing it next to her left ear. I switched the scalpel to my right hand and moved my body until I was sitting on her legs, then sliced her black shirt down the middle.

Her breasts were on full display, and the exhilaration I should have felt was not there. I felt for her uterus, and with precision, carved my diamond-shaped strip of flesh.

Now, Charlotte would heed my warning. She would know she was being watched.

Chapter 16

My freakin' head was thumping, and I felt like I was going to vomit. I pulled my face from the sticky bar top, wondering how the hell I had gotten here. Then I remembered the damn tequila shots. I looked around, and the bar was empty. Where the hell was Jessica?

I yelled out for her, and oh, God, my head. I placed my hands on my temples, cursing the tequila. When Jessica didn't answer, I stood from the bar and grabbed my bag. I looked around again, and the place was deserted. I checked the locks, and the back door had been left open. Dammit. She must have left me here in her drunken state. I hoped she made it home okay. It was three in the morning, and she'd forgotten to lock the door. Anyone could have walked right in while I was passed out. Shit.

I'd only agreed to a few shots because of what had happened with Greg and Heather Finley. My heart hurt, and I just wanted to forget. Now, I was regretting those damn drinks. I needed water and greasy food. I called out for her a few more times, but when she didn't answer, I went ahead and left out the back door, locking it behind me and then sending her a text to let me know she had made it home safely.

Then I thought of Nicky. Shit. I hadn't heard from her. I scrolled though my phone as I stumbled home. I kept having to hang on to the side of buildings to stop myself from falling. Drinking had been a very bad decision. I sighed in relief when I read that Nicky had made her way to the hospital safely, and Randy was doing all right.

I finally made it to my building and climbed the two flights of stairs to my apartment. I was really going to vomit. There was a reason I never drank straight tequila, and this was it. When I opened the door, I threw my things on the floor, completely missing the table, and slammed the door shut behind me.

There was no way I was making it to my bed. I crawled onto my couch and grabbed a throw blanket. Just as I was about to close my eyes, I looked up.

I screamed at the top of my lungs. Someone had been in my apartment. Scrawled in red, and in what looked like blood, were the words:

YOU'RE NEXT!

I sat straight up and went in search for my phone, shaking like a leaf. I had to get out of here. Oh, my God. The words looked like they'd been carved into my wall, with blood dripping from them. I was gonna be sick.

I found my phone, threw open the door, and ran down the stairs to the curb. I couldn't call Nicky; she was with her brother. Who the fuck could I call? I was pissed at Greg, but damn. He was the only one I *could* call right now. I dialed his number.

Before he could say a word, I screamed into the phone, "Someone broke into my apartment, wrote something on my wall. I need the police here now. I need you here now. I can't. I don't know. I can't. I'm fuck. I can't. I can't breathe."

I was having another panic attack.

"Char, I'm calling it in, and I'm on my way now. Be there in five."

I dropped the phone onto the sidewalk. I couldn't breathe. I hugged my knees, rocking back and forth, trying to control my breathing. Nothing was working. Who would do this to me? And why? The copycat killer? Francis's accomplice? Had he not done enough by killing my parents, and nearly killing me?

I threw my head in my hands and wailed. I couldn't control the sobs that escaped me. I wanted my mom, but she was dead. I wanted my dad, but he was dead, too. Because *he* had killed them. I had no one. I felt so alone. I couldn't do this. I couldn't live like this anymore. Not without them. Why? Why! I was so lost. Never-ending despair consumed me—my heart, and this time, I couldn't fight back. Where was my strength? Where was the old Charlotte? Why couldn't I find her? Why? This was all too much to bear. God! My heart!

I needed to get angry, but I couldn't. Not right then. Maybe it was the tequila, or just maybe, I'd been through too damn much in the past month, and I'd had enough. I couldn't just suck it up and deal. It hurt too fucking much. Everything hurt too much. And now, someone else wanted me dead. Well, fuck them. They could get in line and take a number.

Greg's screeching tires caused me to look up. I saw his black BMW pull up to the curb, and he jumped out. "Char! Hey, come here." He picked me up off the curb and wrapped me in his arms. "I'm so sorry for what I said earlier. I didn't mean it. I'm just stressed, and I'm an asshole." He continued hugging me, then pulled away and wiped my tears.

"You are an asshole, but thank you for coming," I said through a choked sob. "Do you have a cigarette? I haven't smoked in years, but I want one."

"Yeah, I keep a 'just in case' pack inside the glove compartment. I'll grab one; it's probably stale, though."

"I don't care. Get a light, too. Then you can go look upstairs." I dried my tears and tried to calm my nerves.

I was breaking down and knew I needed to call my psychiatrist tomorrow after the will. Damn. The reading of the will was in less than five hours, and there was no way I was sleeping in my apartment. Shit. I would have to call Nicky and see if I could stay in hers. She was gonna flip her lid.

"Here." He handed me a cigarette. "This is gonna kill ya, ya know." He grimaced. "Sorry, bad joke."

I put the cigarette in my mouth. "Gimme a light, will ya?"

He lit my cigarette, and I nearly choked. But I was determined to smoke that damned thing. I sent Greg upstairs, sat my ass down on the stoop, and waited for NOPD to get there.

I called Nicky and gave her a summarized version of what had happened. And just as I suspected, she freaked the hell out. Who could blame her? She said her brother would be fine without her, and she was on her way home. I told her to stay, because I had a key to her place, but no. She was having none of it. She was pissed. Once she got something in her head, there was no talking her out of it. So, I reluctantly agreed.

Blue-and-whites were swarming my place, and I was actually happy when Nicky showed up. She ran upstairs, demanding Greg let her get some of my things, so I would have clothes to wear tomorrow. I thought for sure someone up there would tell her no because they were still processing the scene, but nope. She came back down with a small suitcase. I was certain she pretty much scared the shit out of everyone.

Nicky set me up in her guestroom, and I'd never been so happy to see a bed in quite some time. I didn't want to talk in detail about what had happened, but I knew I'd have to tell her everything tomorrow, or later today. It was already tomorrow, and I had to get up in three hours.

I threw myself onto the bed and fell asleep instantly.

***

I walked through the front doors of my parents' home, hearing the sound of my mother's voice. How was this possible? Was I dreaming again? My heart filled with joy at the

167

thought of seeing her lovely face—and my dad! I could hear him laughing.

I ran through the foyer toward the kitchen. Mom and Dad were sitting at the kitchen table looking through an old picture album. I couldn't find my voice. They were here, and alive. All I could do was stand there and stare at them.

"Look, Dan"—Mom pointed to my high school graduation picture, standing alongside Heather Finley—"they were so young, and had their whole lives ahead of them. I can't believe they're really gone." Then Mom began to cry, and Dad wrapped his arms around her.

I ran toward the table in a panic. "But Mamma, I'm not gone. I'm right here." Neither she, nor Dad would look at me. "Daddy, I'm here."

Dad dried the tears from Mom's face and looked into her eyes. "We'll see our baby girl again someday. Have faith, Leanne. She wouldn't have wanted to live the way he left her." And my dad broke down into tears. My dad. I'd never seen him cry.

I stood there in shock, watching them, unable to utter a word. My parents were alive, and they thought *I* was dead. How could this be happening? Was I really dead? Had everything that was going on in my life been my own personal hell? Was I living in some kind of warped afterlife? Purgatory? Was I paying the penance for not heeding my mother's warnings and pleas to quit homicide? No! I couldn't be dead. It could *not* be true. This had to be a dream.

"If she would have only listened when I asked her to quit working homicide, then just maybe..." Mom threw herself over the photo album and wept, her shoulders heaving in racking sobs.

I couldn't take anymore. I stepped closer to the table and tried to touch her, but my hand went right through her head. I jerked back and stared at my hand with my mouth hanging open. What the hell was going on?

"Mamma! Daddy! Look at me. I'm not dead. I'm right here. Please, just look at me." I fell to the floor on my knees, looking at them, pleading, and crying. "God, please let them see me. I'm not dead. Please, just let them see.

"Please don't leave me all alone. I need you. Mamma, can you hear me?"

They continued to sit at the table as if I wasn't in the room. My heart was breaking all over again. How could they not see me? I needed them now more than ever.

I slammed my fists onto my thighs. "Please, Daddy! Look at me!"

Francis Medley's voice broke through my screams, and my heart stopped in my chest. "Little birdie, little birdie—let's play a game. Charlotte, sweet Charlotte—they can't see you, and you only have yourself to blame."

I shut my eyes, throwing my hands over my ears, shaking my head, and then screamed at the top of my lungs, "Nooooo!"

I screamed until my voice was hoarse, until I couldn't take another breath. When I opened my eyes, the scene before me—my parents, their home—shattered, like small broken shards of glass all around me.

I opened my mouth, but no sound would come out. I was surrounded by pitch-black nothingness that had no beginning and no end. Nothing, not even a sound could escape it. I couldn't even hear my heart as it galloped in my chest. I was completely and utterly alone.

***

"Char! Wake up! Oh, my God, wake up." Someone was shaking me, but I couldn't stop crying, and I didn't want to open my eyes. My mom and dad thought I was dead. I saw them, and they couldn't see me, or touch me. Why? I *needed* them desperately.

I was so lost inside my own head, I had no idea where I was. "Char!" Someone shook me harder this time. Was that Nicky's voice? I needed to open my eyes. Oh, God. I'd had another nightmare.

I slowly opened my eyes. "I'm awake," I choked on a sob. "I saw my mom and dad, Nicky. But..." I just couldn't. I couldn't say anymore. I didn't want to relive that dream.

"Oh, honey. I heard you screaming and crying. I've been trying to wake you up for five minutes." She pulled my head into her lap, pushing my sweaty hair from my face. "You scared me. I'm so sorry. I hate this, all of this. It kills me to see you go through such torment."

I looked up at her horror-stricken face. If she only knew. I was lucky to have someone who cared about me so much.

"I—it felt so real. I thought I was..." I closed my eyes and sat up in the bed, wiping the tears from my face. "I can't do this. I can't talk about it. I'm sorry."

"Shh. It's okay," Nicky said. "You don't have to say a word. Is there anything I can do?"

Make it all go away. "No, not really. What time is it, anyway?" I looked around the room for a clock, but my vision was still blurry from crying.

"It's around six forty-five. Do you want to reschedule the meeting with your attorney? I can call him if ya want." She looked so sad and concerned. I hated feeling like such a burden.

"I need to get it over with, and I really want to go to Mom and Dad's. I should have gone after the funeral." I hung my head, thinking about all of the things I'd forgotten. All of the responsibilities a daughter was supposed to handle when her parents died. I'd barely been able to get their funeral together.

"All right. I'll get everything set up in the guest bathroom, so you can get ready. Coffee's in the kitchen." She squeezed my hand and left the room.

I sat there for a long moment, analyzing everything I'd been through: the attack, my parents' murder, nightmares, and now, a copycat murderer, killing my friend, and stalking me. I'd had enough! I was *not* going to be weak. I may still be healing, and my heart shredded, but I was by no means a woman who ever backed down from a fight.

I was done crying. I was done feeling sorry for myself. I was done with it all. It was time I *did* suck it up and deal the best way I knew how. *Get angry.* And that's exactly what I did.

I would continue to see Georgia, but in the meantime, I was going back to work. I was going to catch that damn copycat killer if it was the last thing I did. After the reading of the will, I planned on calling Captain Davis to discuss just that. He might disagree, but I knew Greg would back me up, and I would make sure we kept Stephanie on the team while I was still healing.

I threw the covers back, feeling renewed. I was taking my life back. I was taking control, and no one was going to stop me.

Chapter 17

We arrived at Jack Flanigan's office at eight o'clock sharp. I could feel Nicky's worried stare settle upon me when we entered the main office. Jack's secretary, Amy, greeted us when we walked in. She was a tall, elegant-looking, dark-haired woman—her makeup was immaculate—with crystal, almost white-colored eyes. I wondered if she was wearing contacts.

"Hello, Charlotte. Mr. Flanigan is on a conference call, but he should be with you momentarily. Please, have a seat." She ushered us toward the sleek-looking lobby, filled with modern-looking chairs, that did *not* look comfortable in the least. Everything was decorated in themes of black and white, with sharp edges. "Would the two of you like a refreshment while you wait? I have green tea, coffee, espresso—"

"Coffee will be fine. Thank you," I cut her off, trying not to be rude, but the list seemed never ending. I turned to Nicky. "What about you?"

She looked extremely uncomfortable. "Same. Black coffee, if you don't mind. Thank you."

Amy nodded with a smile, wearing her high-priced Chanel suit, and you could hear the click-clack of her heels as she walked across the marble floors. She returned a few minutes later with our gourmet coffee.

"Here you go." She handed us our cups. "If you need anything at all, I'll just be over there."

"Thank you," Nicky and I said in unison. This place was so stuffy. I was ready to do this thing and get the heck outta here. The expression on Nicky's face said she felt the same way.

We sipped our coffee in uncomfortable silence, glancing around at, well, black-and-white everything. When, finally, I saw Jack appear from his office. Thank God.

He walked toward us, and we stood. "Charlotte." Jack extended his hand in greeting. "I'm sorry it's taken so long to get everything in order, but there were a few snags along the way. Nothing to worry about, though. I took care of it." He released my hand. "Are we ready to proceed?"

"Yes," I said almost too loudly. I felt my face light up a bit, and I could hear Nicky attempting to hide a snicker next to me. I wanted to kick her.

We walked into his window-encased office. How did he have any privacy in here? Oh well, it was none of my business. There was a huge black marble desk resting near the far wall, with built-in bookshelves behind it. The view from the sixteenth floor was mesmerizing, looking out over the whole of downtown New Orleans.

Jack motioned for us to sit in the black leather chairs opposite him as he slid into his seat behind his desk. "As I'm sure you're aware, Charlotte, you are the sole heir to Dan and Leanne's estate. There are a few legalities we need to go over before I go into the reading of their Last Will and Testament. Do you have any questions before we proceed?"

I shook my head. I had no idea what to expect and just wanted him to get on with it.

"Very well." Jack steepled his hands together on the desk. "Your parents had a sizable estate, and because of this, and the nature of their death, their life insurance company had to perform an investigation."

"What?" I interrupted him. "They were murdered. What was there to investigate?" I felt the anger inside of me begin to rise to the surface, but I attempted to push it back down.

"It is standard procedure, but as I said earlier, I handled it, and now you will need to sign a few documents, as you are the sole beneficiary." He opened a file, withdrew several sheets of paper, and slid them across the desk. "I've indicated where your signature is required with tabs—here, here, and here. If you wish to read over it, that is fine."

"No, no. I'll just sign it. Do you mind if I borrow a pen?" He handed me a black pen, and I leaned over, flipping through each page, signing each document. When I was done, I passed the paperwork back to him.

Nicky sat still as a statue next to me, not saying a word, which was unlike her. I was surprised she didn't insist that I read each word of the insurance claim.

"All right, the will. It is very brief. Would you like me to begin, or do you need a minute?"

"Please continue." I could feel myself growing agitated with the formalities, but knew it was necessary.

"The Last Will and Testament of Dan and Leanne Pierce..." I zoned out when he read their names.

I heard bits and pieces about the house and all its contents belonging to me, and when I heard the sum of four million dollars, I stood from my chair.

"Wait. What? Did I just hear you correctly? Four million? That can't be right. Mom and Dad didn't have that kind of money."

"A large sum, in the amount of three million, was left to you in a trust from your birthparents, Michael and Ava Hernandez, to be awarded to you upon your thirtieth birthday, or in the event of the untimely death of your adoptive parents, whichever came first."

I sat back down in my chair, dumbstruck. My parents had never told me. Was this why Mom had wanted me to get out of homicide, because she knew I would have a much better life coming to me in the form of a trust fund? I couldn't believe it.

"Charlotte. Are you all right?" Jack asked.

"Yeah. Shocked is all." I ran my hands through my hair. "What am I supposed to do with all that money?"

"I can set you up with an accountant who will help you invest it wisely. That would be your best course of action. As for everything else, your parents' home, and all of their belongings, they're all paid for."

"Okay." I was numb. Holy crap. It didn't matter. It was just money. I could donate some of it to help abuse victims or help people in need. That was more money than I would ever need in a lifetime. "Is that all?"

Nicky laughed, and I looked at her. "What?"

"Is that all? You have four million dollars, and you just asked if that was all. It struck me as funny. Sorry. I'm in a bit of a shock over here. Just ignore me."

I shook my head. "So, what do I need to do now, Jack?"

"Sign here." He pointed to what I assumed was the will. I was in la-la-land. I signed where indicated. "I'll be in touch when the money is routed to your bank account. Do you want it all in savings for now, at least until you've discussed your options with an accountant?"

"Sure. You have my information." I was still in a daze. Holy shit. This was insane. My birthparents had left me money. I couldn't wrap my mind around it.

Jack stood from his desk. "Well, that's all I have for today, but if you have any questions, please don't hesitate to give me a call." He reached out to shake my hand. I shook his back, my arm feeling like a limp noodle.

"Thanks, Jack. Talk to you soon." I kicked Nicky's chair to get her attention.

"Oh, right. Nice to meet you, Mr. Flanigan." She stood, shaking his hand, and then we beelined it for the door.

When we made it back to my Tahoe, Nicky was as dumbfounded as I was. She was sitting behind the wheel, looking straight ahead. "Do you want to head over to your mom and dad's house now, or wait until later?"

"Well, I really need to talk to Captain Davis first, and then I'll go. I've decided to go back to work."

"What?" She turned her head, staring at me in shock. "Are you serious? After everything?"

"Yes. Very serious. I made up my mind this morning. I'm not allowing fear to rule me anymore, and I want to help bring this murderer to justice. He killed my friend, Nicky." I shoved my hair out of my face. "I can't sit by and do nothing anymore. If anything, I'll be a consultant, but I have to do something."

"But, Char, I know I can't stop you, and I'm glad to see part of the old you back, but you need to consider the ramifications of what this might do to you. The nightmares." She reached over and squeezed my hand. "And what happened last night. Someone was in your apartment."

"And that's exactly why I'm doing this. I will *not* back down and cower in fear. Not anymore. I've had enough. It's time I put on my big girl panties and do what I can to help. I'm done being afraid."

"All right, I support you no matter what. I hope you know that, but I don't want to see you get hurt. You can stay with me as long as you need to."

"About that. I was thinking of staying in my parents' house now. I'll make sure the security system is up and working, and this way, I'll feel safer. No one will be breaking in there."

"If that's what you want. Whatever you need me to do, just ask." She switched on the engine and headed toward her apartment. "I'll drop myself off, so you can go to the station."

"Okay. I'll let you know what they say."

***

When I arrived at the station, I went straight to Captain Davis's office. I didn't stop to talk to anyone; all they did was stare open-mouthed, anyway. I had no time to discuss what had happened to me, or if I was doing okay. I was on a mission.

I knocked on his door twice, and then entered. He was on the phone, and when he saw me, his mouth dropped open in what looked like shock.

"I'll have to call you back," he said into the receiver and then hung up the phone, still staring at me. "Detective Pierce, are you all right? Stevenson told me what happened in your apartment last night."

After closing the door behind me, I took a seat in front of his desk. "I was shaken up, but I'm fine. It's part of the reason I'm here. I want to come back to work. I won't be a sitting duck for some psycho, when I can be out there looking for him instead."

The captain opened and closed his mouth several times, like he didn't know what to say. He cleared his throat and then took a drink of coffee. "Charlotte. You've only just begun to heal. I don't know if you're ready. And what about counseling?"

"I'm getting better, and I'm seeing Georgia, and will continue to see her. I need this, Captain." I leaned forward, placing my hands on his desk, pleading with him. I wasn't going to take no for answer, even if I had to beg.

He looked toward the ceiling, then ran his hands through his thinning salt-and-pepper hair. "Have you talked to Detective Stevenson about this?"

"As a matter of fact, Greg has come to me a few times, off the record of course, but at the time, I didn't think I was ready. Now I am. I know he'll support me coming back to work." I leaned away from his desk and placed my hands in my lap. "I do have one request when you allow me to come back: I want Detective Hamilton to stay on as his interim partner until I'm fully healed. Even if that means I only work in a consultant capacity."

"I'm surprised to hear you say that. But I'll take it under consideration. Let me talk to Detective Stevenson and Dr. Henderson, and I'll call you later tonight."

I stood from my chair, looking him straight in the eyes. "Captain, with all due respect, I'm ready, and I'm willing to do whatever it takes to put this copycat killer behind bars. I refuse to be a victim any longer. I'm a detective, so please, just let me do my job."

The captain sighed and ran his hand over his face. "Under one condition: you work as a consultant with both Stevenson and Hamilton at all times. I don't want you working alone." He leaned forward and picked up a pen, clicking it back and forth. "You're in no condition to be returned to full duty, and you can't argue that, but I understand your need to get back to work. Desk duty is all I can allow."

Shit. It was better than nothing. "I accept. Thank you, Captain. I'll call Greg and find out where we are on the latest murders."

"And what about your apartment?"

I didn't want to think about that. "Once the scene is processed, I'm moving out, and into my parents' house. It won't be an issue. I realize I can't officially work on that part of the case, but I can go over any details that might have been missed."

Captain Davis stood from his chair to see me out. "This is where you must tread carefully. The killer seems to be centered around you, and we can't have any loose ends, or anything that could be considered tampering of evidence that would lead to a mistrial once the perp is apprehended. Understood?"

"Understood, Captain."

"I want you here tomorrow at noon. You'll work in the situation room until I give further instructions. I'll have the casefiles brought over in the morning."

"Thank you, Captain. I appreciate this."

He reached out to shake my hand. "Be careful, Charlotte. I'll see you tomorrow." He opened the door for me, and I walked out, taking the long hallway toward the stairs leading to the parking lot of the rear entrance.

This was it; I was finally taking my life back, one case at a time.

Chapter 18

When I turned on the engine, I looked down at my beeping cell phone in the console, seeing four missed calls from Nicky. I panicked, thinking something had happened to her brother Randy in the hospital. Snatching up my phone, I quickly called her back. On the first ring, she answered.

Nicky was screaming and crying into the phone. "Char! Oh, my, God! She's dead!"

My heart thumped wildly in my chest. "What? Who's dead? I can barely understand you." *Another murder... Not again.*

"Jessica! I found her in the bar... In the bathroom," Nicky shouted, and it sounded like she'd hit something.

"Nic, have you called the police? Where are you now?"

I couldn't believe Jessica was dead. I'd just seen her last night. We were just working together at the bar. My heart... This couldn't be happening.

"I'm at The Styx. Greg and Stephanie just got here."

"I'm on my way. I love you. Please, don't leave their side."

"I love you, too, Char. Oh, my God." She continued sobbing, and I heard the line click.

I tossed my phone back into the console and pressed my face in my hands. I could feel the panic rising in my chest; my heart was beating a hundred miles an hour. Why would anyone want to kill Jessica? I lifted my head when everything started to fall into place. The killer was targeting people close to me, just like he had when he'd murdered Heather.

I didn't understand Jessica, though. We barely knew each other. Was he now getting desperate? Oh, my God. Had Jessica gone back to the bar after I'd left? She never called, or returned my text, but then the killer had been in my apartment. Was he was looking for *me*? Did he think he would find *me* in the bar because I wasn't home? I knew then that I needed to get to The Styx and talk to Greg and Stephanie as soon as possible. What if he'd killed her because of me? Son of a bitch!

I sped toward the bar as quickly as possible, weaving in and out of traffic. I couldn't believe I'd been so stupid. I should have never drunk that much, and made sure Jessica got home okay. I wasn't going to allow myself to fall into another pity-party, but I would take responsibility for my actions.

I banged my fist against the steering wheel, willing the traffic to move. It was barely going at a snail's pace. I needed to be there for Nicky, and I needed to talk to Greg, and tell him what had happened last night. If I wouldn't have been so sloppy-ass drunk, I might have thought to say something then. But how could I have known if she went back to the bar? Shit!

When I finally turned onto Saint Charles Boulevard, the street was swarming with police, and I could see the forensics team going in. Dammit. I pulled into the parking lot, shut off the engine, and jumped out of the truck, running toward the door.

Nicky was sitting just outside smoking a cigarette when I rounded the door. "Hey, honey." I knelt down beside her; she was a wreck, trembling from head to toe.

"Char, it's so bad. Jessica... I—I've never seen..." She trailed off.

I hugged her. "I'm so sorry. I can't believe this happened. I need to talk to Greg and Stephanie. Are you gonna be okay right here, or do you wanna go in with me?"

"I'm just gonna sit here. I already gave them my statement." She inhaled her cigarette and looked down at her feet; tears were flowing down her face and onto her shoes.

"All right, hon. I'll be back in a few minutes to check on you. If you need me, just yell." I didn't want to leave her sitting there; it killed me, but I had to talk to Greg.

She could only nod as tears continued to fall down her face. My heart hurt for her. I could only imagine what she'd seen. Now, I was going to have to see it for myself. *Jessica...*

I walked through the back, seeing Greg and Stephanie talking to a uniformed officer I didn't know.

When Greg saw me, his face was grim, and he shook his head, stepping away from the officer. "Hey, Char. I don't think you should be here."

"It's all right. I talked to the captain, and I'm going back to work tomorrow—as a consultant—but that's not what I want to talk to you about. You need to know about last night."

We walked closer to the bar where we could have a little bit of privacy. "What is it? What happened?"

I told him how Jessica and I had stayed after closing the bar and decided to drink a *lot* of tequila. I shamefully explained how I'd passed out, and when I woke up at three a.m., she was gone, but the back door had been left unlocked. I showed him the text I'd sent, so he could mark the time, and told him to pull my phone records if needed. This way, it might help establish a time of death.

I gave him my theory about the possibility of Jessica coming back after I'd left, and how I thought the killer might have been looking for me, considering what had happened in my apartment. It was quite possible he had killed her while the department was processing the scene in my living room. I wasn't exactly sure about the timelines, but I knew in my gut, they would most likely match up. It sickened me to the core because I hadn't been there to protect her.

"Char, this is bad. What if he would have come in here while you were passed out? That girl in there could have been you." Greg scrubbed his hand over his unshaven face and leaned against the bar. "It's the same fuckin' signature, except this time, her tongue was removed like two of the Medley victims. Unless details of those murders were somehow leaked to the press, or Francis has an accomplice, I don't see how this killer would have known. The wounds are identical."

I took a breath, and then another, remembering what I had put together on the Medley case—foreboding, sinister, the right hand of God, the semblance of truth, trustworthy.

He freakin' knew the victim, just like Medley. Maybe he *was* working with Medley in the beginning, and now, striking out on his own as a copycat. It all made sense. I was the one who had gotten away. I lived. So, in some perverse manner of speaking, he was going to make me pay with the lives of those around me.

I explained all of this to Greg just as Stephanie walked up to us. "I remember your notes on the case," Stephanie said. "You're absolutely right. How else would the killer know such intimate details, and why would he be stalking you?" She turned and folded her arms against her chest. "And your apartment; the warning. It seems he may have been looking for you and found Jessica instead. This is fucked up."

"At least we have a starting point now," I said. "We know who he's looking for and might be able to pinpoint who he'll target next." I looked toward the back door, and my heart dropped to my feet. "Nicky. We have to keep her safe. If he's targeting me, or people closest to me, she'll be next on his list. I can't allow anything to happen to her."

"I'll take her home," Stephanie offered.

"Thank you." I nodded, stuffing my hands in my pockets. "I'll be there in about ten minutes. There's just a few things I want to talk to Greg about first."

"All right. See ya in a few." Stephanie walked through the back to get Nicky.

I was attempting to rein in my panic as thoughts of someone harming her raced through my mind. She was literally all I had left. I had to catch this guy before it was too late, or he killed someone else. I still couldn't believe Jessica was dead.

"Are you sure you want to see the body?" Greg asked. "I can take you back there, but she looks... It's just really bad. It's possible she was using drugs just before she was killed. We found trace amounts of cocaine on the counter, and paraphernalia on the floor next to her body. They'll have to run a tox screen to be sure, but by the looks of it, she was definitely using."

I could feel my insides shaking, feel the blood running through my veins. "Yes. I need to see her. I'm going back to work tomorrow, and I'll see the photos anyway."

Greg cleared a path, so we could walk through to the ladies' room. The forensics team was still processing the scene. I thought I was going to be sick when I saw her severed tongue resting beside her left ear, the same cut down the left side of her face, and the diamond-shaped pattern that had been sliced from her abdomen. She'd been strangled and left out on display like some kind of... I couldn't. I had to turn and walk away, holding my stomach.

I'd process the photos after. I knew it would be easier to separate myself then, not remembering how I'd just been with her the night before. This never should have happened.

Greg touched my shoulder when I walked away from the crime scene. "Are you all right?"

"Yeah... No, but I will be. It's just hard seeing her like that." I dropped my hands to my side and dug my keys out of my pocket. "I'm gonna head on over to Nicky's. I have to be in the office tomorrow at noon. See ya then."

I didn't wait for him to say anything. I just turned and walked out of the bar.

***

Nicky was bundled up on the couch with a soft pink blanket, sipping coffee when I walked through the door. Stephanie was sitting next to her, rubbing her back and talking to her in soothing tones. I had a whole new respect for her now. I couldn't thank her enough for taking care of my best friend at a time like this.

When Stephanie looked up, I smiled. "Thank you for getting her home. Do you guys want me to get you anything? Are you hungry?"

Nicky was still shaking when she spoke. "I don't think I can eat anything, but thank you." The look in her eyes seemed lost and far away. I knew that look all too well.

"I'm okay," Stephanie said. "If you don't mind, I'm going to meet up with Greg and see what else we can do today."

"All right. I'll see you guys at the station tomorrow." I set my keys on Nicky's side table. "The captain said I could do desk work as a consultant. So, I'll be helping you with a few cases."

"It'll be nice to have you back." Stephanie stood from the couch and then looked down at

Nicky. "You have my number if you need anything, okay?"

Nicky nodded but didn't reply. It seemed she was still in shock, and who could blame her? I was afraid she would never be the same after what she'd seen.

I opened the door. "Thanks again, Stephanie. I really appreciate everything you've done."

She smiled at me. "We take care of each other; it's what we do." She leaned in and whispered, "Try to get her to eat something if you can. She hasn't eaten all day, and I'm afraid the shock of everything has just been too much for her."

"I will."

Stephanie turned and walked out of the door, and I closed it behind her.

Taking a deep breath, I looked at my friend. She seemed so far away, and I knew I had to do something to help her.

Sitting beside Nicky on the couch, I wrapped my arms around her. I knew she wasn't the affectionate type, but right now, she needed me. She buried her face into my shoulder and cried. I smoothed her blonde hair and let her get it all out. My heart was breaking with each racking sob. I'd never seen her in so much pain. She had been the one holding me together. Now it was my turn.

"We'll find the mother fucker who did this, Nicky. I promise you that."

I knew I shouldn't be making promises, but I was determined to find that sadistic piece of shit, even if I had to die trying, and I would protect Nicky with my life.

All of a sudden, Nicky jumped up from the couch, throwing her blanket to the floor. "I can't do this. I'm *not* doing this. I'm not going to sit here and cry." She angrily swiped tears from her face. "I'll help you find him, Char. I may not be a cop, but now it's fucking personal. He was in your apartment last night, and he killed Jessica. I am done! No one, and I mean *no one* fucks with my friends." She stomped toward the kitchen, and I heard her throwing things around.

I followed her into the kitchen to see what she was doing. She pulled a 9mm Beretta from the second drawer next to the fridge, and then a box of ammunition, setting it on the counter.

"Nicky, honey, do you know how to use that thing?" Her eyes were wild and laced with anger.

"My daddy taught me how to shoot as soon as I was old enough to hold a shotgun. Hell, yes, I know how to use it." She loaded a clip and slammed it in place.

"All right. I was just checking." I feared I needed to tread lightly here. Nicky was on a rampage, and one I didn't want to be on the receiving end of.

"We're going to the gun range. Now. Get dressed." She looked down at herself. "Scratch that. I'll get dressed. You wait, and I'll be right back."

"Yes, ma'am." I was *not* going to argue with her on this. I needed the practice, anyway. And, well, she needed to let out some of that rage. It was a good plan for both of us.

Chapter 19

Going to the shooting range had been the best idea Nicky could have thought of. I had no idea how therapeutic it would be for the two of us. She screamed in frustration, allowing tears to fall freely, as she hit each target with one hundred percent accuracy. Damn, I was impressed. I'd never seen this side of her, but it was good to know if we were ever attacked, I would have someone just as skilled with a weapon as I was.

Each target I shot, I imagined Francis Medley's face. I realized it wasn't exactly healthy for my state of mind, but if not for him, none of the events from approximately the past year would have happened. And my parents would still be alive. And just maybe, we wouldn't have a stalking-ass copycat killer on the loose, attempting to drive me crazy and make me his next victim.

Firing the last round in my chamber, I looked to Nicky. "You about ready to call it a day?"

She removed her hearing protection, giving me a funny look, and I had to ask her again. "Yeah," she said, setting her gun on the table between us. "I think I've done enough damage for one day, but damn, that felt good."

I agreed. "It was definitely a good way to relieve the stress of the past month." I slid my gun back into its holster. "You gonna be okay?"

What a stupid question. I wanted to slap myself. I only hoped she didn't have recurring nightmares like I did.

"Yeah, I think I will. My heart just hurts, ya know? I've known Jessica since she was a kid. I've been trying to keep her off drugs for a long time and thought working at the bar would be good for her. She'd been in and out of foster homes, until she ran away at seventeen." Nicky shook her head. "I had no idea she was still snorting that shit up her nose, after being clean for five years. I saw it in the bathroom, Char."

"We have no idea what was going on in her life, hon. Everyone has their vices, and maybe she had some shit going on she just couldn't get past, and felt it was her only way of dealing. Ya just never know."

"I know you're right. It just hurts is all. She was a good kid." Nicky packed up her gun and put it back in its case, along with the extra ammo she'd brought along. "Let's get outta here and grab some food. I'm starving."

That was good to hear. "Ya wanna go to my parents' house? We can stop at the grocery and pick up a few things. Mamma always loved her industrial kitchen. It'll be nice cooking in there again, maybe feel like she's with me."

I knew that sounded a bit morose, but I wanted to go home desperately. I needed to be around their things. See their faces in pictures, and just be...

"Oh, Char. Of course. Whatever you want. Do you mind if I spend the night there with you tonight? I don't want to stay at my place. I just can't..."

"Seriously, Nicky. You needn't even ask. We'll grab some of our clothes, food, and head on over there. It's on the way."

Nicky walked over and hugged me tightly. "I don't know what I'd do without you. I meant what I said: you're the sister I never had." Her eyes went wide. "Shit. Randy was supposed to get out of the hospital today, and with everything that was going on, I forgot to call him."

"It's all right. I know he'll understand. You can call him while we're on the road."

She took a deep breath and exhaled. "Thanks for this."

"Anything for you, Nicky. You know that." I nudged her. "Now move that skinny ass. It's getting late, and I don't want to be at the grocery when everyone and their cousins decide to show up."

She laughed at me and pushed my shoulder. "Come on, Miss Badass. Let's go."

We piled into my Tahoe, and Nicky called her brother as soon as she clicked her seatbelt. He was at home resting, and only worried about her safety, asking if she'd be going back to work. That was a good question, one I'd be asking when she hung up.

After she ended the call, I asked about the owner, Tom, and if he'd been notified.

"Yes, and he's closing down the bar until the police are done cleaning up the...mess." Nicky looked out the window as I drove through the city traffic. "I don't know how I'm supposed to go back to work in there after this, knowing what happened. Johnny is, well, he couldn't even come down to the bar. He was so upset. Even after Greg told him he needed to see him for questioning. Johnny only agreed to meet him at the station."

"I can't say that I blame him." I kept my eyes trained on the road; traffic was getting heavy again. "I hate that you were the one who found her."

Nicky sniffled a little but straightened in her seat. "Yeah, it was bad, and not something I ever want to go through again."

We found a small Mom-and-Pop grocery store just off to the right and decided to shop there, instead of a bigger chain. It would be less crowded. Nicky picked out shrimp, smoked sausage, and all the fixings to make gumbo. We grabbed some coffee, teabags, and some sugar to make sweet tea, too. It sounded good to me. We were in and out in no time at all. I hated shopping.

Pulling into the apartment complex, Nicky ran in, packed a bag, and grabbed the one I already had packed. She was back within five minutes. I'd never seen a woman pack and move so fast.

My parents' home was located just on the outskirts of the city, standing on a large two-acre estate. Neighbors were spaced far enough away where there was always a sense of privacy.

When we pulled into the winding driveway that circled in front of the house, I felt my heart plummet. But when I looked around, I noticed the manicured lawn and landscaping had been maintained all this time, and I wondered who had kept it up. The church? I hadn't been around to ask, or even pay anyone to do it.

The three-story, yellow Antebellum home was a beautiful sight with grey shutters, and a walk-up front porch where Mom and Dad's white rocking chairs sat untouched. If I closed my eyes, I could still see them having their morning coffee, reading the newspaper, just as they always did every morning.

We stepped out of the vehicle, grabbing our bags, and walked toward the front steps. My heart threatened to beat out of my chest, but I knew it was only due to my nerves and not stepping foot inside this house since before... just before.

I set my bags down and then pulled the keys from my pocket, but when I went to turn the lock, the door swung open. "Nicky, stand back!" I had no idea who had been in my parents' house, or if someone was in there now. *Fuck, not now. Not here.*

Nicky grabbed her gun from its case and told me to shut the fuck up. Alrighty then. I guessed we were going in together. I pulled my cell phone from my pants pocket with my other hand, and hit Greg's number on speed dial, just in case.

Nicky and I searched the entire house, and no one was there, but it had been cleaned; not

203

a speck of dust, or even a dirty dish remained in the house. Who the hell had been in here? As far as I knew, no one else had a key except me. Then it dawned on me—the insurance company—my parents had been mur—died here. A cleanup crew had been called in. I realized I was losing my shit and forgetting everything I knew as a detective. I wanted to slap myself. Again.

"Nicky, put your gun away; it's fine. It was only the cleanup crew. They must have forgotten to lock the door. I'll bitch to the captain about it tomorrow. I'm a damn idiot."

"Far from it," Nicky said, stashing her gun into the waistband of her pants. "I would have flipped, too. Shit. After everything that's happened, you're allowed to be on guard, Char. Stop beating yourself up. Damn."

"Yeah. I should remember these things, though. It's like my mind is drawing a total blank when it comes to procedures I should know like the back of my hand. Good thing I'm going to work tomorrow." I pulled up the handle, dragged my bag past the parlor, and looked up the polished hardwood stairs. "You can sleep in the guestroom if ya want. I'm gonna take my old room."

"That's fine. I don't care right now. I need food." She went straight to the kitchen and started unloading the bags of groceries onto the bar. I guessed she was cooking.

I'd guessed right. Nicky wouldn't allow me to cook a thing; I just sat at the bar and watched, and the smell was heavenly. I did make us some sweet tea, though. It had been a long time since I'd had it. I remembered—it was with Mamma, in this very kitchen. Feelings of nostalgia washed over me, and I left the kitchen and went to the family room.

Pictures of us as a family sat atop a white hand-carved mantel. I touched each one, staring at our smiling faces. We were so happy then. There were pictures from our trips to the beach, my high school graduation, and when I graduated the academy; my dad looked so proud. Both Mom and Dad were kissing my cheeks in that picture. I swiped an errant tear when I pulled the picture from the fireplace mantel. That one was going to sit on my bedside table in my old room.

I heard Nicky call out that dinner was ready, breaking me from my trip down memory lane. It was fine. I felt at peace, and in some small way, I could feel my parents watching over me. I only hoped they would still be proud of me.

As I walked back toward the kitchen, I brushed my hands along the side of Dad's ratty old maroon recliner that Mom had hated so much. She'd threatened him daily that she was going to take it to the dump while he was gone, but she never had the heart to do it. I smiled to myself at the thought of their little tiffs. They had been so much in love, and they loved me. I was blessed to have had them in my life, even for such a short amount of time.

Dinner was perfect, topped off with sweet iced tea. I couldn't have cooked it as well as Nicky, so I was grateful she had taken over. I was more of a "pop it in the microwave" kinda gal. I did know how to cook. I just never really had the time with my schedule. I ate until my stomach threatened to spill over my waistband. Nicky wouldn't even let me do the dishes. I wondered if she was just busying herself to keep from thinking of what had happened today. I honestly couldn't blame her.

I was exhausted and told Nicky I was headed upstairs to take a shower and go to bed. I needed a good night's sleep before work tomorrow, but I insisted on at least cooking breakfast in the morning. She nearly growled at me but relented in the end.

I checked the locks—the security system wasn't up and running again yet, but I'd handle that tomorrow—then made sure she knew to take the room next to mine before I got ready for the night. It was nearing ten p.m., and Nicky was still downstairs. I was becoming increasingly worried about her, wondering if she'd be able to sleep.

After I was showered and dressed in my night clothes, I looked around my old room; it was exactly the same as I had left it when I moved out. Mom never changed a thing. All of my high school memorabilia hung on the walls, and then I saw a picture of me and Heather on my dresser the day of our high school graduation.

I picked up the picture, looking at her beautiful face; it was hard to believe that she was dead. I'd never gotten the chance to say goodbye. I needed to go visit her family. I needed to fight for her, her kids, and all the other voiceless victims who'd been killed.

I set the picture back on my dresser, willing myself not to cry. I would not shed another tear until that sadistic fuck was behind bars. Then I would cry tears of joy for the families of the victims who would finally have closure.

I climbed into my four-poster princess bed and smiled. It was pink. I pulled the covers over me, and within a few minutes, I drifted off to sleep.

***

It was my high school graduation day, and I was standing next to Heather Finley. We were laughing and joking about the after-party Drake Winters was throwing tonight. Everyone from our class was going to be there, but Mom had insisted I didn't need to be going to parties where there would be drinking involved, saying it was too dangerous, and I was too young.

"Mrs. Pierce, there won't be any alcohol," Heather said, "and Drake's parents will be there. It's just a graduation party, and Char can spend the night with me. He just lives down the road."

Mom looked at her suspiciously. "Heather, I wasn't born yesterday. I know how teenagers are, and I know they sneak alcohol into these kinds of parties."

"Oh, come on, Leanne. She only gets to graduate from high school once. Let the girls go and have some fun." Dad looked at me pointedly. "But if I hear of you getting drunk, college bound or not, you will be grounded until the day you leave."

Heather and I jumped up and down. "Thanks, Daddy!" I threw my arms around his neck and kissed him on the cheek.

"Dan, you're such a pushover," Mom said smiling. "Come here and give your mamma a hug. Please, be careful, Char." She hugged me tightly. "We love you."

I waved goodbye and left in a hurry with Heather beside me. "Love you, too, Mom and Dad. See ya tomorrow!"

Heather and I took off toward her red convertible Mustang parked near the curb. "I can't believe they fell for it," she said. "Did you bring a change of clothes?"

I buckled my seatbelt. "Yep, they're in your backseat."

"We need to hurry." Heather glanced over at me. "Everyone who's anyone will be there within an hour or so."

"Let's get a move on, then."

I could feel the wind whipping through my hair, and I felt free. I couldn't believe we had finally graduated, and I was going to Drake's party! I was so excited. I'd had a secret crush on him since sophomore year.

We stopped at Heather's house for about fifteen minutes to change our clothes and refresh our makeup, and then we headed over to Drake's house. By the time we got there, the place was packed full of cars. The only place to park was in his yard or up the hill. We parked as close as we could, jumped out, and smoothed our short skirts, checking each other's makeup and hair at the same time. Perfect.

We marched up the long driveway to what looked like his mansion on the hill. I'd never been in a house so big. It was a huge home that looked as if it was built from creek rock, with nothing but windows lining the front. A large set of stairs led to the double-doored entrance.

When we walked in, loud music thumped in our ears, and it was filled with wall-to-wall people from our senior class. Heather and I made a beeline straight to the kitchen, wading through the throng of our classmates, where four beer kegs were set up near the patio leading to the backyard pool. The center bar had numerous bottles of whiskey and rum scattered from end to end, with red disposable cups wrapped in plastic sleeves.

Heather handed me a cup, and I poured myself a shot or two of straight whiskey, then took a long drink. It burned badly going down, and I almost spit it back out.

I turned to Heather who was about to take a drink, but the skin on her hand started melting. I screamed, "Heather!" I knocked the drink from her hand, and then she looked at me. "Your hand. Look at your hand!"

In the next moment, Heather's red hair turned to blood; it dripped onto the floor and ran down her face. Her hazel eyes were unseeing, and cuts appeared all over her face and arms. Crimson gore spread all over her body, covering her clothes; the flesh from her arms and legs began to fall to the floor in bloody heaps.

I couldn't find my voice. I looked around for help, but everyone was gone. It was just me and Heather, standing in Drake's kitchen all alone.

I took a step back when her tongue fell from her mouth; she was just standing there in a daze, as if she felt nothing.

"Heather," I whispered, covering my mouth with my hands.

I was dreaming again. This had to be another nightmare.

Heather's body crumbled to the floor; a large gash on her left cheek appeared, and I screamed at the top of my lungs. I needed to wake up. I didn't want to see anymore.

"Heather, nooo!" I closed my eyes, willing myself to wake up. Then I heard a familiar voice.

"Little birdie, little birdie—let's play a game. Charlotte, sweet Charlotte—nothing is the same."

I dropped to the floor, closed my eyes, and covered my ears. I would not play this game. I rocked and prayed to wake up.

"Little birdie, little birdie—"

"*Shut the fuck up!*" I'd had enough, and I was waking up from this nightmare. He had no control over me.

I opened my eyes, and Heather was gone. I was alone. Francis's voice was gone. I picked myself up off the floor and stumbled toward the front door.

Chapter 20

I awoke with a start and sat up ramrod straight in the bed, breathing like I'd just run a marathon. My heart was beating frantically in my chest. Hot tears threatened to spill from my eyes as images from that horrific dream flashed in my mind. When would this ever stop? I needed to pull myself together.

I looked around the room, and it was still dark outside; the light from the moon shone through my window. I had no idea how long I'd slept. I grabbed my phone from the bedside table, and it read 3:33 a.m.

I knew I needed to go back to sleep and get some rest if I planned on being worth a crap at work today. However, thoughts of closing my eyes again caused panic to rise in my chest. I guessed it was going to be an all-day coffee day to keep me awake. It wasn't like I hadn't done it before.

I couldn't get the visions of Heather's body out of my head and decided to get up and wash my face. Throwing my covers to the side, I climbed out of bed and walked to my en suite bathroom, then flipped on the lights. Blood was running down the white-tiled walls, and I threw my hands over my mouth to cover my panicked scream. I closed my eyes, knowing it wasn't real; it was just another hallucination left over from the nightmare I'd had. Just like before.

I needed to talk to Georgia. This had to end.

I kept my eyes closed for several moments before opening them. When I did, everything was back to normal. I sighed in relief and wasn't sure my heart could take anymore. I'd have to call Georgia today before I went into work. Taking control of my life meant also learning how to cope with my nightmares, without freaking the hell out each time. I knew it would be a long process, but I had to do something about it sooner rather than later.

Turning the cold water on, I splashed it on my face, waking me even further. I grabbed a towel from the wicker basket sitting on the counter and dried my face and hands, deciding to get dressed for the day.

After I pulled on a pair of black pants, a white cotton, long-sleeved button-down shirt, and my black boots, I headed downstairs to make some coffee. When I reached the bottom landing, I heard light snoring coming from the family room, knowing it was Nicky. She'd never made it to bed.

I walked into the room to find her curled up in a ball on the couch; she'd left a small light switched on from the lamp sitting on the side table. I picked up a cream-colored throw blanket from my dad's recliner and covered her up. She looked peaceful, and I didn't want to wake her.

I tiptoed from the room, careful not to step on any creaking hardwood floorboards, and made my way to the kitchen. I turned on the small light above the stove to make a carafe of coffee.

Sitting on a barstool, waiting, I thought about what Nicky had been through, and my heart ached. I remembered having to sleep with a light on for years and being afraid of the monsters lurking in the dark. I hoped she didn't have to go through what I did. No matter what, I knew I would be there for her.

The coffee began to percolate in the carafe, making a damn racket. I hadn't thought about the noise, and then I heard Nicky stir in the family room. She sluggishly walked into the kitchen, joining me at the bar.

"Hey, why are you up so early?" She yawned and nearly fell off the stool before she sat down.

I didn't want to tell her I'd had another nightmare, but she'd know if I was lying, especially at four a.m. I never got up this early unless it was for a case.

I looked at her and mumbled, "Another nightmare, but it's fine. Nothing I can't handle."

"Ya know, this may not help now, but I used to have them a lot after my parents died. It went on for years, Char. It's nothing to be ashamed of." She pulled me to her side and one-arm hugged me. I wasn't expecting that.

I knew her mom and dad had died in a car accident years ago, but we'd never really talked about it much.

"I'm sorry, Nicky. I didn't know." I laid my head on her shoulder. "I wonder if that damn coffee is ever gonna make itself."

She laughed at my attempt to change the subject. "Listen, I didn't like to talk about it because it was too painful, but I had Randy, and we made it through." She stood from the bar and grabbed two mugs from the counter, pouring us some coffee, setting a cup in front of me. "I had to go through years of therapy myself, something I've never told anyone except Randy."

My mouth fell open. "I didn't—this is why you insisted I see someone, huh?"

"Yep." She slid back onto the barstool and blew on her hot coffee. "Now it's time I tell you why." She took a deep breath, closing her eyes for a moment, and then looked at me with a few tears sliding down her face. "Char, I tried to kill myself after it happened. If Randy hadn't found me when he did, I wouldn't be sitting here with you right now. The nightmares were so bad, I couldn't tell dream from reality, and I wanted it all to end. We're not so different, and that's why I'm telling you this now. Stop trying to hide from me. I know, even when you don't tell me."

I set my coffee mug on the bar top and stared at her, open-mouthed in shock. I couldn't believe this, that she had dealt with the same feelings and emotions that I was currently going through now. I knew there were others out there, and I wasn't special, but my Nicky? I had no idea.

"I'm sorry I've kept things from you. I felt like such a burden after the attack, and well, my parents, and you were doing so much for me already. I just didn't want the only person left in my life to run screaming."

I had laid all of my insecurities out on the table, bared my soul, but now, I knew that she understood.

"That's where you're wrong. I would never leave you, and you were never a burden. It's time you stop thinking of yourself in such a way."

I nodded, taking a sip of my coffee. "Thank you for telling me. I know it must have been hard."

"No, not as hard as watching you go through this without knowing and understanding that you're not alone." She turned in her seat. "I should have told you from the beginning, but I was too afraid to say it out loud myself. That's on me. Now, we can get through this together, and no more secrets. Got it?"

I tried to smile. "Got it. I'm going to call my psychiatrist today before work and tell her about this latest nightmare. It was gruesome, and about Heather from back when we were teenagers." I closed my eyes, willing the images to go away.

"I'm sorry, Char. Things will get better in time, but the pain, it only lessens, and you learn how to deal with it one day at a time."

***

Nicky and I talked for a long time, eating a small breakfast, that she'd prepared—I lost that battle—and at nine a.m., I decided it was time to see Dr. Henderson. I would call on the way, but I was determined to see her today, even if I had to wait. I dropped Nicky off at her car and told her to go back to my parents'—my house—if she wanted. She could stay as long as she needed.

Driving toward Georgia's office, I connected my phone using my Bluetooth, and when I said her name, it dialed the number to her office. The receptionist answered, and I asked to speak with Dr. Henderson, saying it was urgent. Thankfully, she wasn't with a patient and took my call right away.

"Charlotte, is everything all right?"

"The nightmares are becoming worse, and I'm going into work today as a consultant. I just need to know if there's anything I can do when they occur that will help me with the aftermath. I can't seem to shake the images, or the emotions afterward."

"This is quite normal, unfortunately. However, there is a medication I can give you to help stop the nightmares from occurring until we can get a handle on it.

"Prazosin is a common drug used for PTSD patients with severe recurring nightmares."

"I hadn't planned on taking any kind of medication, but if you think it will lessen the nightmares, then I'm all for it." I could hear her rustling some paperwork around.

"All right. Just stop by here on your way to work, and I'll give you the prescription. We'll monitor the dosage and see how it works for you. Make sure you keep our scheduled appointment for Wednesday."

I breathed a sigh of relief. Finally, something to help me. "Thank you, Georgia. I'll be there in a few minutes to pick up the prescription, and I definitely won't be missing our session. I have a lot to talk about."

"That's good to hear, but Charlotte, I want you to know, you can call me anytime if things get too bad. I'll leave my personal number with my receptionist."

I couldn't believe someone who didn't even know me was so willing to help me.

"I can't thank you enough. I, I don't know what to say, except thank you."

"No thanks necessary. This is my job, and I want to see you living your life the way you want to, and not in fear. I'll see you soon."

"Bye, Georgia."

We ended the call, and I finally felt like I could take a deep breath without the normal panic that ensued. I would have to thank

Captain Davis for referring her. I knew if I continued seeing Georgia, my life would become my own again.

After picking up my prescription, I dropped it off at the nearest pharmacy and headed into the station about an hour and a half earlier than the captain had expected. When I walked through the front doors this time, I had a smile on my face. I felt like I belonged again, like I was part of the team. And just maybe, this was what I had been missing while I had been blaming everyone around me for something neither I, nor they, had any control over.

First, I knew I had to forgive myself, and then forgive them. Surprisingly, I had, and I didn't even realize it until I went to my old desk, seeing Stephanie's smiling face.

"Hey, Char! It's so good to see you." Stephanie stood from her chair and wrapped me in a tight hug, then looked into my eyes. "You're early, and that's perfect. I have some things we need to go over as soon as you're ready."

"It feels good to be back." I pulled away from her; she was still smiling, and it was infectious. "I just need to talk to the captain first if he's not busy."

"He's talking to Greg about the latest case, but I'm sure he won't mind if you go on in." I turned to walk away, but she stopped me. "Oh, and the captain had all the casefiles delivered to the situation room for you earlier this morning."

"Okay, thanks," I said, and then walked toward the captain's office down the hall.

I knocked a few times and waited. I didn't want to barge in on their conversation. Greg opened the door with a frown, but when he saw me, his face lit up with surprise.

He opened the door wide for me to walk in. "Hey, Char. We were just talking about you."

"I hope it was good things." I laughed, seeing Captain Davis sitting behind his desk, still looking like he hadn't slept in days.

"Well, your apartment has been cleared and cleaned," Greg said, closing the door, "so you can go in and get your things when you're ready. We're just waiting on the forensics report for any fingerprints, and DNA from the blood that was on your wall."

"Okay. Thank you. I just wanted to let you know I'm here and ready to get started wherever you need me."

Captain Davis leaned back in his chair. "As I mentioned before, I need you to be careful when reviewing these casefiles. Most of the victims knew you—and Jessica Paris—you were the last person to see her alive."

I sat down in the chair, folding my hands together. "What are you saying, Captain?"

"Only that if the FBI is brought in, you'll be the first one they look to as a suspect. I know what happened that night, and the man we presume to be the killer broke into your apartment, but we need a solid case, and all of the forensics to back it up."

I opened my mouth to say something, but I knew he was right. It was standard procedure. I *was* the last person to see her alive. It didn't matter that I was passed out drunk; the only person who could account for my whereabouts was Greg, and that was only after I'd learned someone had broken into my home. The only thing I did have was a text message, asking Jessica to call or text me, to let me know she'd made it home safe.

"You have my phone records showing the text message I sent, along with Greg's report. That's all I can say. It'll be what it'll be. I have nothing to hide, Captain."

"I know, Detective. I just wanted to give you fair warning, especially after what happened with Medley. You don't need any more shit on your plate."

"I was with her, Captain," Greg said. "If it comes down to it, I'll vouch for her. I saw the blood, and the message left on her wall; we have evidence that someone was in her home. Her life was threatened. Not to mention, Medley's own words, and a copycat who seems dead set on stalking her."

"Thanks, Greg. I appreciate it, but we need to let everyone do their job, as the captain said. If we don't have a solid case, even the slightest slipup could allow a killer to be set free. I'm not willing to have that hanging over my head. I'll cooperate and do what I can to help."

The captain stood from his chair. "I'm glad you understand, and you're not taking it personally. Every single one of us wants this case solved, and it's good to have you back on board." He looked to a red-faced Greg. "Show her to the situation room, and Charlotte, you sign nothing—only consult and take notes, handing them over to Stevenson or Hamilton."

"Yes, sir." I stood from my chair and followed Greg to the situation room.

As soon as we walked in, Greg shut the door. "This is bullshit. Under no circumstances should you be looked at as a suspect. Hell, you almost fucking died!"

"Greg, it's fine. I get it, I do. It's all part of the job. Just let it go, all right?"

"Fine, but I won't allow anyone to railroad you." He ran his hands through his dishwater-brown hair. "Want some coffee?"

"God, yes. The whole pot."

Greg left the room, and I sat at the conference table, looking through a few casefiles, saving Heather's for last. I'd already seen it, and after my dream, I didn't want it to be the first one I opened.

I set the casefiles aside for a minute and decided to look at the whiteboard. This had always been the best way for me to separate myself from the victims and attempt to piece together the similarities, to find anything that might be missing.

The first victim: a blonde female—another found in Audubon Park—staged almost exactly the same as the last Medley victim. Her face was unrecognizable due to the multiple lacerations; she had more than one gash along the left side of her cheek. Her mouth had been sliced, looking as if she were wearing an eternal smile; this was different, unless I counted my mother. But I wasn't going to think about that.

There was another deep incision on the right side of her cheek as well. It made me wonder if this victim had been a test, or if she'd fought back. I'd need to look into the casefile. The same diamond-shaped pattern of flesh was expertly cut from her abdomen, and she'd been strangled like the others. There was something familiar about her, but I couldn't quite put my finger on it.

The second victim was Heather, and I had to close my eyes and take a deep breath. I'd seen the photos; I just needed to keep a clear head. Her wounds were exactly the same as the Medley killings, no deviations, except for one: she'd been left in New Orleans City Park, naked. However, according to preliminary reports, there were no signs of sexual assault. It seemed the killer wanted to humiliate her in some way. It was personal.

Which brought me back to my original theory: he knew the victims. The first one had to have fought back, making him angry, so he butchered her face, making an identification near impossible without DNA or fingerprints. I needed to look at the autopsy report.

And the third, Jessica Paris. I already knew the scene. I couldn't wipe it from my memory if I tried. Her tongue being removed did hold significance, though.

I went back to the casefiles and began flipping through the first one. When I saw the name of the first victim, I felt like I was going to vomit. Stacey Boudreaux. We'd gone to college together, but, like Heather, I hadn't seen or spoken to her in years. I had to get out of that room and get some air. This killer was targeting anyone who had a connection to me, either from my past, or present. I needed to call and check on Nicky.

Chapter 21

When I stepped out of the situation room, Greg nearly knocked me over. I just walked past him and ran for the front door. Nicky was all I could think about. I'd left her all alone. What if something happened to her while I was at work? I couldn't think about that. I pushed my way through the doors, and quickly dialed her number.

"Hey, Char."

"Oh, my, God. Nicky—where are you?"

"I'm at your place. What's wrong?"

"I just found out who the first victim was. And I knew her, too. I..." I was about to have another panic attack, and shit! I didn't want it to happen on my first day back.

"Hey, calm down and take a deep breath, okay? You knew this would be hard. Just listen to the sound of my voice and breathe."

"I am." I sat down on the front step, looking up at the clear blue sky.

"I think you might be too close to the case. You need to do what you always do and separate yourself. But first, if you haven't already, you need to tell Greg, or someone, that you know this victim."

"Okay, but I just needed to make sure you were safe. Nicky, he's targeting anyone who's close to me, and that means you. I can't lose you." I felt the tears coming but sucked them up.

"I know, and I have my gun on me at all times. I'm at your house, and I'm safe. No need to worry about me, all right?"

"Easier said than done. Just let me know if anything strange happens and keep all the windows and doors locked."

"I will, hon. Now, get back in there, breathe, and tell someone what you just learned. It's the only way you're going to work through this."

"Okay. Just call me later; let me know you're all right."

"I will, Mom." I could hear her holding back a laugh.

"Ha-ha, not funny. Seriously."

"Promise, now take your ass back to work."

"All right. I'm going in now. Talk to ya soon."

I ended the call, but my heart was still racing. This was insane. I was being stalked again. I already knew as much but seeing it on paper made it all the more real. It pissed me off and scared the shit out of me at the same time.

I walked back through the bullpen to find Greg and Stephanie headed my way; both had worried expressions on their faces. I didn't say a word, only motioned for them to follow me into the situation room.

We walked in, and I shut the door behind us, pointing to the photos of Stacey. "I know her. We went to college together, and I didn't recognize her at first, but... I know her." I plopped down in a chair. "I haven't seen her since we graduated from college. This is fucking bad. Why her? And why people who know me? I don't understand the logic behind any of this."

Stephanie sat beside me and squeezed my hand. "We know he's been stalking you. It could be a number of things, and we never know the method behind the madness of a serial killer until it's over, and sometimes, not even then."

Greg was standing off to the side, not saying a word. He looked even more pissed than before.

"He deviated with the first—with Stacey." I looked toward the board. "He knows them all. He has to, either that, or he's been watching them closely for a long time. None of this makes any sense anymore."

I looked at Greg. "Do we have any of the forensics reports back yet? DNA? Anything?"

He took a seat opposite me and shook his head. "We only have preliminary reports from the first victim. We're still waiting for everything else."

"Well, shit. What kind of leads do we have? A profile? Something to go on, so we can go out looking for the son of a bitch?"

"Char," Stephanie interjected, "everything we have so far is centered around you, because you knew most of, well now, all of the victims."

"So, what are you saying, that he's trying to set me up? For fuck's sake, I was in the hospital and then with Nicky for weeks. What the hell?"

"No, I'm not sure, only that he's making this all about you. This is what I wanted to talk to you about earlier, *before* you went over the reports and found it for yourself."

I crossed my arms on the table and put my head down. Who the hell was doing this to me, and why?

Greg touched my arm. "Char, it's going to be all right. We'll find him. As soon as some of the DNA reports come in, I'm positive something will turn up."

"All right," I said through my arms, head still on the table. This sucked. I wasn't sure how much help I could be right now.

Screw that. I picked my head up and stood, smoothing my hands over my pants.

"Okay, I'm not wallowing. Let's go over what we do know. Who's gonna take notes?" Stephanie volunteered. "All right. Look at the first victim—the differences—and, Greg, check the casefile to see if anything was found beneath her fingernails. I have a feeling she fought back.

"Greg, also look for any evidence of sexual assault. The other two victims' bodies were staged in a way to humiliate them. I need to know if the first was the same."

"On it." Stephanie began taking notes as Greg spoke.

"Greg, any residue beneath her nails?"

"We're still waiting on DNA, but it looks like there might have been traces of blood and skin; we can't be sure until the results are in."

"All right, well, that's a start," I said. "This gives us an idea that she did, in fact, fight back, and why her murder was more brutal than the others.

"Stephanie. What of the victims' families? Did they notice any kind of strange behavior, or did they mention anything about someone following them to their family members? Husbands? Sisters? Friends?"

"According to reports, the only person who thought someone was stalking her was Heather," Stephanie said, "but she never filed a report. Her mom said she'd been receiving threatening phone calls during the night."

My heart stopped. "Just like Ginger Walters, and my mom and dad. It's the same signature as Medley. Could this have been a warning? Did Heather ever tell her mom what the caller said?"

"Only called her a whore and warned her to change her ways, or something like that," Stephanie said. "I'd have to check the report for specifics."

"Fucking asshole has some kind of God complex, just like Medley." I walked back to

233

the table and slid into my seat. "Remember how I said there was some connection between 'the right hand of God,' and Medley possibly using some slight he felt against God to rid the world of what he felt was unclean or unjust?" I looked between the two of them. "We could be dealing with the same kind of crazy here. Do we know if Medley attended church in the past, and if so, where, and, was he close to anyone? This is where we might find our perp."

Stephanie nodded her agreement and stood from her seat. "I'll get right on it. This is a good start, and we might just find the lead we've been looking for. Great work, Char."

"Look for surrounding churches in his neighborhood," Greg told her. "I'd say he would've stayed close to home."

Stephanie looked at him before closing the door. I could feel the tension in the room going up a notch. What he'd told her was a given. Stephanie already knew what to do, and she didn't need him to tell her, but I kept my mouth shut, opting to choose my battles wisely.

"Greg, please go over the casefiles, both the Medley killings, and the copycat murders; see if anything jumps out at you." I stood by the door and looked at him. "I'm going to get authorization to check the call records for Heather Finley and see if there's a link to Ginger Walters. They were made from a burner phone originally, but this guy might have slipped up, and possibly used a different method."

"All right, use my computer. If you find anything, let me know."

"Will do." I turned and shut the door behind me.

When I walked back toward Greg's desk, I saw Johnny's huge frame and dark brown, spiked head come into the station. He was wearing a tight white T-shirt and faded blue jeans. I didn't know he was supposed to be interviewed today.

He saw me, giving me a half smile. I went to him and asked who he was here to see.

Johnny put his hands in his pockets and looked down at his feet. "Detective Stevenson called, saying he needed to ask a few questions and take my statement."

"Okay, I was just with him. Do you want to have a seat while you wait?"

"Char, I don't know if I can do this. I don't know anything, except the last time I saw Jessica, she was still alive. It's just all so..." He trailed off, looking over my head.

"I know, Johnny; it's awful. I still can't believe it, but we're gonna do everything we can to find the person responsible, all right?"

He nodded and then took a seat in the waiting area.

I squeezed his shoulder, feeling terrible that he had to go through this, too. "I'll be right back."

I went back to the situation room and let Greg know he was here. I wondered why he hadn't told me that he would be interviewing Johnny today.

I watched as Greg led him to Interview Room Number One, and the look on Greg's face was strange; it bothered me. Was he still holding a grudge because Johnny had threatened to throw him out after he'd upset me at the bar? I hoped not.

I walked over to where Stephanie was making calls. She'd just hung up the phone. "Hey, did Greg tell you he was going to interview, or take Johnny's statement today— for the Jessica Paris murder?"

Stephanie looked up at me in surprise. "No, he didn't say a word about it. In fact, he hasn't said anything about the guy."

"Huh. Well, Johnny said Greg called him this morning, telling him he had to come to the station and answer some questions. Do you think he's looking at him as a suspect without informing us?"

Stephanie pulled her blonde hair into a ponytail. "It wouldn't freakin' surprise me. He hides shit all the time."

"That pisses me off. Nicky told me Johnny would have to come here, but she didn't elaborate, only that he refused to go to the bar because of what happened." I sat on the edge of her desk, folding my arms and looking down the hall. "Ya think we should listen in? Greg had a look on his face that I didn't like. And I'm sure he forgot to mention that Johnny almost threw him outta the bar the night of the murder for pissing me off."

She looked livid. "What the fuck did he say to you?"

"He showed me Heather's casefile and basically told me I needed to suck it all up and do my damn job. I yelled and told him to get out. That was about it, but I lost my shit."

"That sorry son of—the nerve of him. I'm sorry, Char. I have no idea why he's acting like this. And you know what? You don't have to suck a damn thing up. Screw him. He has no idea..."

She looked down at her at hands, and I wondered if maybe she'd been through something similar. I could see she was holding back tears, but I didn't pry. It was none of my business. Stephanie and I, it seemed, had a lot more in common than I thought.

"Hey, it's fine. I can deal with Greg. Let's go see what's happening in there."

She stood and nodded; then we walked to the two-way window room, so we could listen in.

When I walked in and flipped on the sound, my mouth dropped open. Greg was holding Johnny by the front of his shirt, yelling in his face.

"I know you killed her, you son of a bitch! And you went back and threatened Charlotte, too! Admit it!" Then he slammed the side of Johnny's face against the stainless-steel table.

"Stephanie, we have to stop him! He can't do this. It's not right. Oh, my God. What the hell is he doing?"

"What the fuck?" Stephanie pressed the call button. "Detective Stevenson. You're needed in the situation room. Now."

Greg looked toward the two-way window and scowled. He'd been caught. He pointed to Johnny, telling him he wasn't going anywhere.

I was freakin' pissed, but I knew I couldn't get involved, not officially, anyway.

Stephanie and I marched our asses to the situation room and waited. Greg slammed the door open. "What the fuck do you two think you're doing? I was interviewing a potential suspect!"

I stepped forward, close enough to where he could most likely smell my breath. "No, Greg. You were beating a witness! Ever heard of police brutality—being sued, you dumb ass? And since when did Johnny become a suspect?"

Greg turned, then punched the wall, and I took a step back. "There are things you don't know, Char. Things in his past that make him a suspect."

"Oh, please, do tell. Stephanie and I have been left in the dark for far too long, and to me, it seems like you're just holding a damn grudge."

"A grudge? Is that what trying to find the person who wanted to kill you, and that murdered the girl in the bar is, a grudge? He fuckin' threatened your life!"

"That girl, Greg, has a name, and it's Jessica. Johnny was her friend. While I understand needing to cover all angles, and taking his statement, I do *not* understand, or condone your attempt at beating the shit out of him without cause."

"And you still haven't told us shit about his past," Stephanie said, all kinds of pissed off. "Not to mention, you leave me out of the loop at every turn, and I'm fucking sick of it!"

Greg threw himself into a chair and put his head in hands. "I'm only trying to protect you, that's all. After what happened with Char..."

"I don't need your damn protection, Greg," she said. "I need a partner I can trust."

The door swung open, and in walked an angry-looking Captain Davis. *Shit.*

"What in the absolute hell is going on in here? The whole damn station can hear the three of you yelling. This is unprofessional and complete bullshit. In my office. Now!"

Chapter 22

I felt like I was doing a perp walk all the way to the captain's office. Greg was furious, and I didn't give a shit. This whole situation was messed up. I'd never seen him act in such a way, and beating the hell out of a witness? That was new. I wanted to know what he thought he had on Johnny that merited beating the shit out of him.

"Shut the damn door. Now," Captain Davis ordered when the three of us filed in behind him. Greg was the last one in, and he closed it behind him.

"Detective Stevenson, I'm going to start with you. What the hell is going on in my department? And you best start talking."

Greg cleared his throat, while Stephanie and I stood with our hands clasped behind our backs. "Johnny Malloy, the bouncer at The Styx, came in for his interview. I've given you information about his past—"

"Wait just one damn minute," I interrupted. "Why not share with your partner, or the team?" I knew I was throwing him under the bus, but after that damn display, I was pissed.

"Detective Pierce. Allow Stevenson to continue. Then you can have your turn to speak."

I nodded. "Sorry, Captain."

"As I was saying, he was convicted and served some time for statutory rape when he was nineteen; the female was seventeen. Somewhat minor, yes, because consent had supposedly been given, but there's more. Upon his release from probation six years ago, and after some digging, I found he had been charged with four counts of sexual assault, but the charges were eventually dropped and never taken to trial, or even before a grand jury. His family paid off the families of the alleged victims."

I couldn't believe it, and I wondered if Nicky knew. I stared at Greg in shock. Why hadn't he told me this? And now I knew why he had a murderous look in his eyes that night at The Styx.

"All right." The captain stood from his seat and looked between the three of us. "Did the alleged victims report mutilation of any sort?"

"Not that I know of, Captain," Greg said. "Most of the records are sealed. That was about all I could find."

"Hamilton, Pierce. What say you?" The captain looked at us.

I had nothing. Not yet, anyway. I needed more information before I could make an informed decision as to whether or not Johnny was a suspect. Just because he had a past, and one we weren't certain of, didn't place him at the scene of all three crimes. We didn't have the evidence to back it up.

Stephanie looked as shocked as I did, but I knew we'd be having a much quieter discussion about this later.

"Nothing, Captain," Stephanie and I said at the same time.

"Very well. Keep your damn voices down and get back to work." He pointed toward the door. "Get out of my office."

We filed out quickly and went back to the situation room.

"Why the hell didn't you tell me, Greg?" I demanded when we walked into the room. "I mean, I was freakin' working there. Not to mention, where's your evidence that he had anything to do with the other two murders?"

"I'd only just found out and wanted to make sure he was the right guy. Everything I have is circumstantial."

"Yeah, based on his past, and the fact that he works at the bar." I shook my head. "While he very well could be a suspect, you need to be careful. You could have just cost us with a damn lawsuit." I had to take a deep breath, because I wanted to punch him. "You don't even know anything about those other cases, except that the women were paid off. You have no details. None. Unless you're holding back?"

"That doesn't explain why you didn't tell me," Stephanie interjected, "or why you're so damn secretive all the time, leaving me out of the loop and not giving me information about new cases. I'm supposed to be your partner."

"Fine. I'm damned if I do, and damned if I don't." He opened the door and looked back at us. "I'm going to finish my interview. Watch if you want."

Stephanie and I looked at each other and shook our heads. None of this added up. Greg was still hiding something; I could feel it, and it wasn't just about Johnny.

***

I didn't stay and watch. I told Stephanie I was going home for the day and needed to check on Nicky. I'd be back at nine a.m. tomorrow. We were hoping the forensics report for the first victim would be in by then. I'd had enough for one day, and Nicky needed to know what was going on.

When I arrived home around three p.m., Nicky was sitting on the couch cradling her gun. "What the hell happened? And why didn't you call me?"

"Someone dropped off a package. It's addressed to you and your parents." She was shaking, and her voice was just above a whisper.

"Where is it?" Shit. This wasn't good. No one knew I was here except Greg, Captain Davis, and Stephanie.

"On the kitchen table." She wouldn't look at me.

"Hey." I walked around to the couch and knelt in front of her. "What's got you so freaked out?"

"There's no return address. Someone knocked about half an hour ago, and when I went to the door, no one was there, or even in the driveway that I could see; just the package. I picked it up and set it on the kitchen table, then blood seeped through the bottom." Her whole body was trembling now. "I grabbed my gun, and I've been sitting in here since."

"Oh, my God. Okay. I'll be right back."

I didn't want to go into that kitchen or see what was in that damn box.

I walked to the kitchen table, seeing a small pool of blood surrounding a rectangle-shaped box. My heart raced, and I knew I had to open it, but first, I pulled out my phone and took a picture.

I grabbed a knife from the drawer, slicing the packaging tape, and when I saw what was inside, I screamed, covering my mouth. There was a stainless-steel scalpel, along with a diamond-shaped strip of bloody flesh, and a note written in blood that said:

YOU'RE NEXT!

I dropped the knife. Still screaming, my hands trembling, I took a picture of its contents and then dialed nine-one-one. I called Stephanie next, and I could barely get out a coherent sentence, just my address, and told her to hurry.

Nicky came running into the kitchen, and I told her to stay away from the package. I didn't want her to see it; she'd seen enough. I had no idea which victim it belonged to, or if it was from another murder.

We waited in the living room for the police and Stephanie to arrive. I kept wondering who the hell would have known to send that shit to my parents' house. Nicky finally settled down a little, and I decided not to tell her about Johnny. It could wait until later.

When Stephanie arrived at the door, I asked where Greg was. She said he'd left right after I did, that he'd let Johnny go.

"Show me the box." Stephanie walked in looking fierce, and I took her to the kitchen, leaving Nicky in the living room.

"Please keep its contents quiet," I whispered. "I didn't tell Nicky, because I don't want to upset her even more."

Stephanie nodded and then peered over at the table. When she saw what was inside the package, she took a step back. "You've got to be fucking kidding me. Char, this is... We need to wait for forensics to get here."

"I know. I took pictures of the box before I opened it." I swiped my phone and then showed her. "I took pictures of all its contents, too."

"Did you touch anything?"

"No, I don't think so, just the box when I opened it. I freaked the hell out, though, then dialed nine-one-one, and you."

"All right. Shit." She ran her hands through her hair and leaned against the bar. "This is sick. We need to find out who this...the blood belongs to, and hopefully we'll find some prints, too. I can't freakin' believe this." She seemed as horrified as I was.

"Keep your voice down." I could hear someone knocking on the front door, and then the doorbell rang. "I think that's everyone else."

"I'll get it. You just go sit with Nicky, and we'll get her statement after that shit is outta here."

"All right. Thanks, Stephanie." I turned to walk away and then stopped. "Hey, have you tried to call Greg?"

"Yeah, he's not answering, as usual."

I shook my head, feeling unease settle in my gut, and then went to join Nicky in the living room. Where the hell was Greg, and why wasn't he here? I wondered if he was still pissed about earlier.

I tried calling him, and he didn't answer me, either. I left a message, saying it was urgent, giving him a brief run-down of what was going on.

"Char, what's in the damn box?" Nicky asked when I walked into the living room. "It has to be pretty bad for half the damn police department to show up."

248

I sighed, taking a seat next to her on the couch. "Don't freak out. Well, never mind. You're gonna freak out either way. All of the victims from both serial killers were left with distinct markings; you saw it on Jessica. The box contains..." I was finding it hard to get the words out. "It has—I'll just call them trophies—from a victim, and we don't know who it belongs to. Anyone could have sent it."

Nicky laid her head against the back of the couch and looked toward the ceiling. "Did you call and get the security system up and running yet?"

"No. I forgot with all the crap that happened at the office today. But I'll call them, and get it transferred to my name and turned back on immediately." I looked at my watch. "I might still have time to do it now. Do you want to go upstairs to my room, instead of sitting down here, watching this shitshow?"

Nicky leaned forward and picked her gun up from her lap. "Yeah, I don't want to be down here when they go through that thing. I'm just thankful no one tried to break into the house."

"All right. Go on up, and I'll let Stephanie know what's going on, so she can find us when it's time for questioning."

Nicky stashed her gun into the waistband of her pants, braced her hands on her knees and stood. "See ya up there."

I went to the kitchen to find Stephanie talking to a short, dark-haired male forensics tech. I didn't want to get in the way, so I just called out that I would be upstairs in my room when she needed me. She looked up with a frown, and then nodded that she heard me. I needed this day to be over.

When I made my way up the stairs, Nicky was standing in the doorway to my room. I nudged her shoulder. "Hey, what is it?"

"It's pink." Nicky laughed, and then began laughing hysterically, holding her side. "It's fucking pink, like Cinderella pink!"

I looked at her like she'd lost her mind, then thought about what had just happened. Well, she needed something to laugh at; my princess room would do the trick.

"Go on in, shithead. The pink princess won't rub off on you." And then I started laughing, too. I guessed laughter was good for the soul after the day we'd had. Or month.

Chapter 22

Nicky and I plopped onto my *pink* bed, after she set her gun on my bedside table, and she was still laughing. I let her go on; she needed it. After finding Jessica's dead body, and then a bloody package, I was certain she was laughing so she wouldn't cry.

I rolled toward her on the bed. "Hey, hyena, are you about done? Wanna go through my high school cheerleading albums and get a good laugh outta those, too?"

"Oh, God! A cheerleader. I can't!" She held her stomach and laughed harder.

I couldn't help but smile. "All right then. While you're enjoying yourself at my expense, I'm gonna step into the bathroom and set up security around the house."

"You do that. I'll just sit here in Pepto Bismol and try not to throw up."

I swatted her arm and stood from the bed. "Shut up. Mom never changed it, and I liked a lot of pink when I was younger."

I walked to my en suite bathroom, shaking my head, and then closed the door behind me. I could still hear her muffled laughter through the door. I was happy she wasn't crying. I guessed this was good. I had no idea.

Nicky was an enigma. One side of her never showed outward signs of affection or emotion, but then after I was attacked, everything changed. She had become so protective, and I'd seen a completely different side of her. She was nurturing and had taken care of me. I'd never had a friend like her, one so genuine who loved me, flaws and all.

I called the security company, Security Alert Systems, and asked that everything be transferred to my name. Surprisingly, it already had been; they were just waiting for my call to activate the monitor. I assumed my attorney had taken care of it, just as he had done with everything else. It was an easy procedure. The system would be up within the hour, and all I had to do was activate it from the downstairs wall unit by the front door.

When I walked back into my bedroom, Nicky was sitting up on my bed—not laughing—clutching a pink pillow. "So, how did it go?"

"Surprisingly easy. It was already in my name, and all I have to do is activate it. Strange, huh? I guess Jack took care of it. I'll have to call and thank him later."

"Yeah, he seems like a good guy." She looked down at the pillow she was holding onto like a lifeline.

"Hey." I sat next to her on the bed. "Wanna talk about it?"

Again, a stupid question, but if she did need to talk, I would listen.

"I feel like you're not safe, Char. Wherever you go, you're not safe, and I don't like it. I'm not worried about me. I can handle myself—"

I cut her off. "I can handle myself, too, and, now we have security here. It's fine, Nicky."

"No, Char, it's not. I need to do something to help, but I don't know what I can do, other than be here for you." She looked into my eyes, and what I saw was loyalty and fierce determination.

"You are helping me. Being with me helps. As much as I love my privacy, I enjoy having you around, especially now that I know you can shoot like a badass." I gave her a half smile.

"Yeah, I can do that. Always could...and it makes me think of my own parents, and what they would do."

"Hey, stop. We're not going to feel sorry for ourselves, remember? We're gonna kick ass and take names."

She smiled at that. "Yeah, I guess you're right. I'll be your backup here at home."

"Exactly. So, chin up. We've got this."

She grabbed my hand and gave me resolute look. "We've got this."

A soft knock at the door interrupted our conversation. "Char, it's Stephanie. Do you mind if I come in?"

"No, it's fine. The door's unlocked." Stephanie walked in and looked around, most likely marveling at my pink room, but she didn't comment.

"So, I just need to ask you guys a few questions before I go. Everything's been taken care of downstairs, so you don't have to worry about that."

"All right," I said. "You can sit in the chair, or on the bed with us, whatever works for you."

Stephanie opted for the cream wing-backed chair to the right of my bed and pulled out her notepad.

"Nicky, I guess I'll start with you. Can you tell me what happened, and if you saw anyone, or anything strange when the package was delivered?"

Nicky took a deep breath and exhaled. "There's not a whole lot to tell, really. Someone knocked on the door, and when I went to answer it, no one was there. I didn't see a vehicle in the driveway, either. I looked down, and that's when I saw it: the package, addressed to Char and her parents."

She looked down at the pink pillow, pulling on a stray fringe. "I picked it up like I would any other package and took it to the kitchen for Char to open later. But that's when I saw blood oozing from the bottom, and I flipped the hell out.

"I ran to the living room and grabbed my gun, then made sure all the windows and doors were locked, and waited for Char in the living room until she got home. I was in a daze, and I didn't think to call anyone. I was in shock."

"All right." Stephanie made a few more notes and then looked back at Nicky. "Is there anything else you can remember, anything that stands out?"

"No. That's it. Char came home about half an hour later, and then she called the police."

Stephanie then looked at me. "I know what you told me, based on the conversation we had in the kitchen. I need you to forward the photos you took to my email; they'll be timestamped. I've already taken a preliminary report from you, and all you and Nicky will need to do is sign them once they're complete.

"In the meantime, just initial and sign here"—she handed us two separate statements—"that this is your true statement, to the best of your knowledge. You'll have to fill out an official statement later, but this will do for now."

Nicky and I borrowed her pen and signed where indicated. I knew tomorrow was going to be a shit day with all this hanging over my head, and then waiting for forensics on the other murders. I hoped we weren't looking at another victim.

"Hey, Nicky," Stephanie said, "remember what I told you before. You have my number, and if you ever need to talk about anything at all, I'm always available. Char knows how to find me, too."

"Thanks, Stephanie." Nicky set the pillow aside, stood from the bed, and hugged her. I was shocked. This new Nicky was, well, I liked the new Nicky—the old one, too. I was happy to see her breaking out of her detached shell.

And it seemed she trusted Stephanie now as much as I did.

"All right, that's all I have for now." Stephanie stood from the chair. "But if anything happens between now and tomorrow morning, call me. I don't care if it's two in the morning, call me."

"We will," I said. "I'll walk you out." I stood from the bed and glanced back at Nicky. "Be right back."

When Stephanie and I reached the front door, I hugged her and then pulled away. "Thank you for coming as quickly as you did. I just wanted you to know that I've reset the security alarm, and it'll be monitored twenty-four-seven."

"I wish it would have been working before, but that's neither here nor there. What worries me is, the killer now knows where you are. Keep that thing on at all times, and I meant what I said: call me if anything happens."

"I'll do ya one even better." I punched the code into the keypad, activating the alarm, and then checked my phone for the link. "Here, I'll send the you link so you can monitor the system yourself, just in case something does happen. I just emailed it to your phone."

"Thanks, Char." Her phone dinged, and she looked down. "Got it. Just take care of yourself, and Nicky. I'll see you in the morning."

"Hey, before you go, do you think I should bring her into the station with me tomorrow? We have to stop by our apartments anyway and grab a few things. Maybe she can run some errands. We can talk to the captain about it and see what he says. The worst thing that could happen is he says no."

"I don't have a problem with it, and it'll keep her safe. I'll call him on the way back to the station and get ahead of it, so you don't have to. I'm sure it'll be fine as long as she's not around confidential information."

"Thanks, Stephanie. I know she'll be happy to hear it. She wants to help, and maybe this way, it'll give her a sense of being part of the team, ya know?"

"Yeah. She's a nice person, and I really like her. You're lucky to have such a good friend, Char." She turned to walk out of the door.

"Hey, Steph. I'm lucky to have you, too."

She smiled and then walked to her car.

I shut the door and heard the alarm chime, letting me know it was engaged. When I turned around, Nicky was standing at the bottom landing of the steps. I wasn't sure how much she'd heard of my conversation with Stephanie.

"So, you think I can help around the station tomorrow?"

Well, I guessed she'd heard it all.

"Yeah, if you want to. I mean, it won't be working on cases, but you might be able to do a few things around the office. For anything else, they'll need to run a background check. As of now, you'll basically be a visitor, but a safe one."

"Can I carry my gun?"

I raised a brow. "That'll be a no. Not into the station, but you can leave it in your car."

"All right, then. Sounds like a plan to me. You hungry?"

"Yeah. Let's head out to town, grab some more clothes, and do some real grocery shopping this time."

She cringed. "I hate shopping, but okay."

"And this is another reason why I love you so much. I hate it, too. In and out. We get what we need and leave."

"Let me grab my stuff, and then we can go."

***

We went to my apartment first. I wasn't exactly sure how I would react going back in there, knowing I could have died if I wouldn't have been drinking at the bar. But I trudged forward anyway. Nicky was beside me the entire way.

When I opened the door, it smelled of bleach and other household cleaners. I didn't dare look at my living room wall, just in case the words hadn't been removed; I had no desire to see them again. Beelining it to my bedroom, I grabbed a large suitcase and threw nearly every piece of clothing I owned inside. I had to get another small bag for extra toiletries and miscellaneous items. Nicky had already thought to pack at least four pairs of shoes, so I was good for now.

Eventually, I knew I would have to come back and clean out the apartment, letting my landlord know I would be moving out, but I wasn't ready yet. I needed to deal with everything else first. This was not my top priority.

Nicky was waiting for me in the living room when I rolled my bags in. "You done?"

"Yep. Let's get the hell outta here."

I still didn't look at that godforsaken wall. I walked to the front door, and after we were out, I slammed it shut, locking it behind us.

Nicky did the same in her apartment. She walked out with three huge bags and was ready to roll. We packed them into the back of my Tahoe and headed for the grocery. I caught her staring at The Styx as we drove by, but I didn't say a word.

Then I thought of Johnny. I knew I needed to talk to her about him, but I wasn't sure how to go about it. Not to mention, it was possible she already knew. None of those charges, excluding the statutory rape charge from when he was nineteen, had stuck, and there had to be a reason why. Something in my gut told me the pieces of that particular puzzle weren't adding up, something Greg was leaving out.

We made it in and out of the grocery in one piece, thankfully, and then headed back to my house. It was almost dark and there wasn't enough coffee on the planet to keep me awake much longer.

By the time we'd unpacked everything, and put the groceries away, I opted for a sandwich, and just wanted a shower and my bed. I was done. Nicky decided to stay up and watch TV for a while, and I made sure the alarm was set before I headed upstairs for my nightly routine.

Showered and exhausted, I fell face first onto my bed.

***

I was lying just inside a concrete tunnel, unable to move. I couldn't catch my breath; someone was choking me. I pulled against the ligature around my neck, but the more I moved, the tighter it became. I couldn't even scream.

I couldn't see. My eyes were shut tight, and when I opened them, I saw the glint of a stainless-steel scalpel reflecting from the moonlight above. My captor's face was cast in a shadow, but I could see him cutting into my shirt, and I knew what was going to happen next. I tried to scream, but nothing would come out.

"Little, birdie, little birdie—let's play a game. Charlotte, sweet Charlotte—scream my name!"

It was Francis. He was going to kill me this time, and I was choking. I bucked wildly beneath him, pulling against the cord, kicking out with my legs. I reached out for the scalpel just before he was about to slice me open. I could feel myself losing consciousness, but I had to fight back. The blade sliced the palm of my hand when I grabbed it, and I kicked again, hitting my mark.

Francis rolled off of me, clutching his balls. I sat up, taking long, deep breaths, holding onto the scalpel, blood dripping from my hand.

"I'm not playing your games anymore! How many times do I have to kill you? Die, you miserable fuck!" And then I stabbed him in the leg. When he reached for his leg, I stabbed him in his groin. Pushing his torso down to the ground, I then stabbed him in the face. I continued to stab him until I had no strength left in my arms, until I felt myself losing consciousness. Blackness surrounded me, and I felt myself falling into oblivion.

Francis was finally dead.

Chapter 23

I awoke screaming and pulling at my throat. When I realized it was only a dream, I was pissed. I'd forgotten to pick up the medication Georgia had prescribed, and now, had another freakin' nightmare, possibly more terrifying than the others. I could still feel myself choking; it was so real.

Nicky came crashing through the door. "Char, are you all right? I heard you screaming."

I could only look at her. I was still horrified, but I knew I needed to get it together; it wasn't real.

"A nightmare…"

Nicky sat on the bed and rubbed my hand. "It's okay. Do you need anything? Water? A shot of whiskey? Orange juice? A shot of whiskey?"

"You said whiskey twice." My voice was still trembling.

"I know. It was a hint." She was trying to make me smile.

"Thanks, but I'll pass on the whiskey." I wiped my sweaty hair from my face. "Francis continues to haunt my dreams, and I kill him each time, but... I almost died in this one. It was awful."

"Hon, I'm so sorry. What can I do?"

"Nothing. It's just something I have to deal with, and hopefully, one day, they'll go away. Maybe when he's behind bars for good? I don't know. Or the copycat is found? Hell, who knows?"

"It's about five a.m. Do you want me to make you some coffee?"

"Yeah, thanks. I'm gonna jump in the shower, if you don't mind."

"Go ahead. I'll meet you downstairs."

I threw my covers back; my legs were still shaking when I stood from the bed. I walked to the bathroom and readied my things for a long hot shower. I needed to wash away the remnants of that damn dream.

I stood under the hot spray until the water ran cold, and then turned the water off, stepping out into the steamy room. I felt somewhat better, but I knew if I wanted to get past this, I was going to have to put it behind me and move on. It was just a dream. It wasn't real.

Getting dressed for the day, I decided to talk to Nicky about Johnny. I knew it wouldn't be an easy conversation, but one that needed to happen, especially if she was going to work with me today. I didn't want Greg dragging Johnny into the station for another round of questioning, leaving Nicky off guard.

I schlepped down the stairs to the smell of freshly brewed coffee, to find Nicky sitting at the bar drinking a cup in silence.

Walking to the counter, I poured one for myself and then turned toward her. "Hey, there's something I want to talk to you about. It's about Johnny." She looked up at me with a strange expression and then nodded.

Taking a seat on the barstool next to her, I continued, "Greg brought him in for questioning yesterday, and... I don't know how to say this." I paused, because I knew how protective she was of her friends. She might lose her shit. "After Stephanie and I stopped him from nearly beating the hell out of him, Greg told us some things about Johnny's past."

Nicky was pissed. I could see it in her eyes, and she slammed her coffee mug onto the bar. "What? No. Wait—why would Greg touch him? He has no right. That son of a bitch!"

"Well, like I said, we stopped him, and then the captain got involved. Apparently, Greg did some digging and found that Johnny has a record; served time for statutory rape—"

"I'm just gonna stop you right there," she interrupted. "I already know this shit. I also know about some trumped up charges that were brought against him from one girl. *One.* He met this bitch at a party while he was on probation and refused to hook up with her." She stood from the stool and began to pace the kitchen with her hands fisted at her sides.

"After he refused her, she cried rape and had her friends join in later. Johnny had a tight alibi for that night; he never left his buddies that night, and never talked to that girl again—she fuckin' left after. All of his friends stated as much, even had pictures to prove it. He had never even laid eyes on the other three!"

"Yeah, I thought there might be more to the story."

"Oh, there is. I'm not done," she seethed, "and if Greg is half the detective he *thinks* he is, he should have known where to look.

"Johnny was just getting back on his feet, and his parents were helping him get back into college. They didn't want a trial like that hanging over his head, because you and I both know, the court of public opinion will always render a guilty verdict, so they paid them off. As soon as those little twits saw dollar signs, they backed off and dropped the charges." Nicky angrily sat back on the stool and drank her coffee.

"Shit." I ran my hands through my still-wet hair. "He said he only had circumstantial evidence, but this is utter bullshit, Nicky. A money trail like that can easily be found. What the hell is he trying to do?"

"Grasping at straws? Blame someone who clearly has done nothing wrong and try to ruin his life?" She stood to pour herself another cup of coffee. Turning from the counter, she looked at me pointedly. "I don't think it's a good idea if I go to work with you today. I can't say that I won't strangle the sorry fuck if I see him. Johnny has worked his ass off, putting himself through college. Hell, Char, this scarred him so bad, he rarely even dates!"

"No, I understand, Nicky, and I'm gonna have a little chat with Greg and Stephanie myself. First things first, I'm pulling the records and throwing them in his face. This is not cool, and not how we conduct a murder investigation."

"Thank you. I don't know how you put up with him." She shook her head. "I really don't. He's a fuckin' asshole."

"It's becoming harder, believe me. Especially after his behavior these last few weeks."

I couldn't believe Greg would cut corners like this just to close a case. I knew in my gut that Johnny wasn't our guy, and now, I had to take time away from the investigation to put Greg in his rightful place. I had no idea what was running through his mind, or why he continued to disappear when Stephanie and I needed him. Shit just wasn't adding up, and Greg was gonna start answering questions, whether he wanted to or not.

"He has been acting strange, and I don't know what his problem is, but he needs to do his damn job. What the fuck was he thinking?" Nicky was still pissed, and I couldn't blame her. Johnny was her friend, and she didn't just hire anyone; she made sure she knew them.

"I don't know," I said, "but I'll get to the bottom of it. I'm heading in early this morning to do just that. When he walks through the door, I'll be handing him a thorough file belonging to Johnny, and then he'll answer my damn questions."

"Good. Punch him in the gut if you can get away with it."

"I might not have to. You should have seen Stephanie going after him yesterday. I'm happy to have been wrong about her."

"Yeah, she's definitely someone you want on your side, especially right now."

Throwing my damp hair into a messy bun atop my head, I poured a to-go cup of coffee for the road. "I'm gonna head on out. If you need anything, call me. And I mean it this time."

She patted the gun I hadn't noticed in her waistband. "I'm all set, chick."

"Gotcha." I gave her a wicked grin. "Don't shoot up the house."

"Shut up, smartass, and go to work. I'll see ya later." She stood and hugged me goodbye.

"I'm going. I'm going." I grabbed my keys and bag from the table in the foyer and disengaged the alarm. "Hey, don't forget to reset this as soon as I walk out the door."

"I'm on it."

"All right. See ya soon." I closed the door behind me, hearing the alarm chime, and then walked to my car.

***

When I walked through the station around seven fifteen a.m., all seemed quiet. I went to my old desk and fired up the computer, hoping Stephanie hadn't changed the password, and she hadn't.

I began my search for Johnny Malloy: assorted charges, statements, indictments, court records, and time served. Many things were even public record. I just shook my head and continued. I easily found the money trail Greg had conveniently left out, and printed everything I had, backing up what Nicky had told me. All of this took me about half an hour. Thirty freakin' minutes. I was pissed.

By the time I had everything in sequential order and placed in a file, Stephanie walked in, seeing me at her desk.

"Hey, Char. What are you doing here so early?"

I quickly gave her the run-down of my conversation with Nicky, and then handed her the file I'd created. Once she was done reading it over, her face went three shades of red.

"He's chasing bullshit leads. This is nothing." She handed the folder back to me. "The guy was innocent, and Greg has nothing on him, except some scenario he's created in

271

his mind. We have to nail this down, Char, before he takes it even further."

"And that's why I'm here so early. I'm not allowing him to railroad an innocent man, when he should be helping us find the real killer. Sure, look into his alibi for the night of the murder, but other than that, Johnny's past is irrelevant."

"Exactly. Speaking of, did he ever call you back last night?"

"Nope. Never heard from him." I stood from her chair. "You?"

"Nothing. Something else we need to talk to him about. This shit is getting old fast."

"I agree." I clutched Johnny's folder in my arms. "Wanna grab some coffee and head to the situation room while we wait for forensics?"

"Sounds good. I need a cup or ten."

After getting some coffee, we went to the situation room. I set Johnny's file on the table and then looked at the board.

"What the hell happened while I was gone? Look at her face!"

The second victim, Heather Finley, had a red X marked across the front of her photo.

"Oh, my God. It wasn't like that when I left yesterday, Char. I have no idea, or why anyone would do that."

I slumped in my chair. "Why Heather, and who had access to this room besides us?"

"The only people in here yesterday that I know of were me, Greg, you and the captain. It's fine. I'll remove it. We have other crime scene photos." She squeezed my shoulder. "Don't let this get to you. We have CCTV cameras in here, and we'll find out who did it."

"All right."

That made me feel better, but I couldn't wrap my mind around the "why." It didn't make any sense, unless someone was trying to make me lose my mind.

Stephanie went through the casefiles and found another photo, removing the one with the X, and then replaced it with the other.

"There. I'll let the captain know when he arrives."

"Oh, and just so you know, Nicky's not coming...for obvious reasons. She was pissed." I gestured toward Johnny's file. "It's for the best. She probably would have throat punched Greg."

"Can't say that I don't want to do the same," Stephanie said. "I'm going to try and call him again. His ass should be here by now."

Another call went unanswered, and a pissed off Stephanie sat across the table from me. "He's ghosting us, Char. Either he knows something, and he's not telling us, or something else is going on. Whatever it is, I'm done."

I had to agree with her. "I've never seen this side of him before, but I'm with you on this. As soon as he walks through the door, we should present him with Johnny's file and go from there."

I grabbed the stack of casefiles and began flipping through them while we waited. I thought I might as well make myself useful, and hopefully, something would stand out, giving us a real lead.

"Hey, were you able to make any kind of connection to the Ginger Walters case; the phone calls to Heather Finley?" Stephanie asked.

I looked up from Heather's file. "No. It was another burner phone, same as Ginger's. But the thing is, everything was the same—late night calls, everything that Medley did. I just wish there was a way to pinpoint the caller."

"Dammit. Wait." She looked at her phone. "I have a message from Sharon in forensics. We might have something on one of our vics. She's sending over a preliminary report now."

I threw my hands up. "Thank God! It's about time."

Just as we were about to get up and go back to Stephanie's desk, Greg walked in looking like shit. He had a black-and-blue bruise on the right side of his face.

"Sorry, I'm late." He walked toward the table and sat next to Stephanie.

"You're just in time," Stephanie said. "Forensics came back, and I think it's on Jessica Paris."

"Good. Now we can nail the prick." Greg started to stand, and I stopped him.

"Before you go nailing anyone, there's something you need to see." I slid Johnny's folder across the table and folded my arms against my chest, attempting to keep my emotions hidden—not very well, though.

"What the hell is this?" He wouldn't open the file.

Stephanie all but shoved it in his face. "Read it, and then we'll talk."

Greg huffed and snatched the file from the table. Once he was done reading it, he tossed it back at me. "So? This means nothing. He could still be our guy."

"Are you insane? You accused the man of killing someone yesterday, Greg!" I stood from the table, placing my hands in front of me. "His past is irrelevant to this case, and he wasn't guilty of shit. Did you even check his alibi for the night Jessica was murdered?"

I was near shouting now, but thought about yesterday, and I didn't want the captain coming in chastising us like children.

"He was in bed asleep. He has no alibi." Greg stood and pointed his finger in my face. "And just so you know, I already have the preliminary reports on Jessica Paris. She was fuckin' killed while your ass was passed out at the bar!"

I gasped and sat back down. "What? How? How could I have not heard someone being murdered...in the... I think I'm gonna throw up." I put my head in my hands, wondering how the hell this could have happened.

"That's enough, Greg." Stephanie jumped from her chair. "You're an asshole, you know that?"

He raised his hands. "What? I'm only telling the truth. You'll see the time of death in the report. She was there, and the killer left her alive for a reason. Then went to her apartment to taunt her. It's fucked up, Stephanie. It's all part of a game to him, and that's why I'm looking into Johnny. He was the last one to see them both."

I raised my head. "So, he killed Jessica while I was passed out, and just... Why not kill me? What's his angle? I..."

Stephanie walked over to me and rubbed my shoulders. "He's dragging this out, as you said before, killing people close to you. We just need to find the 'why.'"

Chapter 24

After the initial shock wore off, I was pissed. This killer was playing a game that I intended to win. He would not make me live in fear. Fuck that. I was done. This only made me more determined to find him.

Forensic reports were finally rolling in, and we were making some headway. Once the DNA results came back, we might just find a match. I knew he would slip up.

Greg walked over to me while I was sitting behind Stephanie's desk. He still wasn't my favorite person right now. "I'm sorry I didn't call you back yesterday. I was working on some things."

I looked up from the computer and directly into his eyes. "What? Johnny, or an actual lead?"

"That's not fair, and you know it." He sat on the edge of the desk. "I'm looking into every possibility, and he's one of them. I know you're pissed, but I want you to know that I put a rush on the package that was sent to your house yesterday."

"Thanks, and yes, I'm pissed. You have no reason to leave me and Stephanie out of everything. It's bullshit. What you know, we need to know, especially her; she's your damn partner, at least until I'm back on full duty. What the hell's gotten into you, Greg?"

"I know, and I'm sorry. There are just some things that I wanted to work through on my own."

"That's not how a partnership works." I could feel my anger rising and tried to tamp it down. I had no idea what he was hiding, but he needed to spill before I took him outside and lost my shit.

"Look, I put a trace on that package for you. I'm trying to see if we can narrow down the post office it originated from. It shouldn't be that hard." He stood from the desk, looking angry. "There could be another dead body out there, for God's sake!"

"You think I don't know that?" I stood and grabbed his arm. "Let's take this outside."

Stephanie rounded the corner just as we were walking out the door. She followed.

"What is it, Char?" Greg slammed through the door and onto the front step. "Do you want to yell at me out here so the captain won't hear? Fine. Go ahead!"

"Actually," Stephanie interrupted, "we would both like a few answers, starting with— why the hell won't you take our calls?"

Greg's face looked murderous, and I couldn't have cared less. "I just told Char, I'm working on some shit. Things aren't adding up, and I'm out beating feet, trying to find the real killer, while you two are in here looking through casefiles."

I thought Stephanie was gonna punch him. "What the hell is that supposed to mean? That I can't do anything except desk work? That I'm only a mere woman and should know my fuckin' place?"

She stepped toward him, inches from his face. "I've worked too hard and too damn long to be treated as less than. I will *not* take this shit from you. I am your partner. You *will* treat me as such, or we'll have a little chat with someone who will make you. Do I make myself clear?"

Greg took a step back. "That's not what I meant. I was just saying... I only wanted to protect... Fuck, what does it matter? If you want to know, fine. I'll show you." He headed toward the door. "Both of you—follow me to the situation room, and don't say shit until I'm done. Then you'll know why I kept you out of the loop."

280

Stephanie and I looked at each other, angry as hell, and then followed him into the situation room.

When we walked through the door, Greg closed it behind us. Stephanie and I took our seats near the far wall.

"Look, I don't want to fight with you two. Just hear me out. I've had some of the preliminary reports for a few days, and I didn't want to share because they look bad. I haven't even told the captain."

Greg pulled up a chair and then grabbed a folder from inside his coat pocket. "Char, you've been through enough, and I didn't want you freaking the hell out. The blood on your wall belonged to Jessica Paris; that's what helped determine the time of death."

"I sort of figured that part out today," Stephanie said. "What else ya got?"

"The killer has personal items of Char's, and how he got them, I have no idea. Again, why I'm looking into Johnny, because he's the closest male, but I haven't found a motive. I might have jumped the gun on that one, and I'm sorry."

"Might have?" I raised a brow.

"Just listen, okay?" He spread out a few more reports. "A necklace you used to wear before the attack went missing from evidence, and it was found near Heather Finley's body."

I sat back and nearly cried. That necklace had belonged to my mother. I was wearing it the night of the attack. Who would have taken it from evidence, better yet, how could anyone without clearance get access to it?

"That doesn't make sense, Greg. How could anyone without access to evidence lockup steal my mother's necklace?"

"This is what I've been trying to tell you. I have no idea. It wasn't signed for, and there's no record of anyone being there on the day of Heather's murder."

"If you would have told me this earlier, I could have helped you dig into it further." Stephanie grabbed the report. "What else does it say that you've been hiding?"

Stephanie's eyes lit up in shock, and then she grabbed another report. "Dammit, Greg. Why would you hide this shit?"

"Because whoever it is, is not only stalking Char, but using her in a way that makes it seem like the murders are some kind of payback. I didn't want you two worrying about this, only working on new leads. And I'm sorry for upsetting you."

I just sat there, knowing this copycat killer had it out for me, and the only reason I could think of was, because I had lived. Why did he leave me alive, though, and still threaten my life? Was he toying with me? He had to be. It was the only thing that made sense.

"Hey, Char, you all right?" Greg broke me from my thoughts.

"Yeah, I guess. I mean, it just is. Whoever this is must know, or at least have followed the Medley case closely. It's the only thing I can think of. We need to find out who stole that necklace."

"I'm on it," Stephanie jumped in. "What else should I be looking for, Greg?"

"I put a rush on the forensics for the package that was delivered to Char's house yesterday. See if they've narrowed down the post office or packaging store where it originated."

Stephanie stood from her chair, taking a couple of the reports with her. "I'm still pissed, but now that I know, I appreciate you finally sharing these reports. We might actually get somewhere with three of us working on it."

Greg didn't say a word; he just looked at me. "I really am sorry, Char. I just didn't want you to worry. You'd already been through so much."

"I understand, but when I chose to come back to work, it was to help, not be left on the sidelines. Just don't leave us in the dark anymore."

Greg left the room, and I went back to the whiteboard where I knew I would be most useful. I was missing something: Stacey.

Why Stacey? And what was the significance? She lived about twenty miles from my parents' home, but I didn't think that mattered. It had to have something to do with our past: college. What was it about our college years that would stand out to someone who was killing people from my past?

Then it hit me. Stacey and I had been roommates in college. She'd dated an abusive guy and ended up getting pregnant. I remembered talking to her about it, going over her options, and asking her if she was sure. Abortion had never been anything I'd ever thought about in my young life, and I was terrified for her, but I'd supported her decision.

She'd asked me to take her to the clinic, and I did. It was one of the worst experiences of her life because of what had happened after. Her ex-boyfriend had found out and nearly beat her to death, landing her in the hospital for weeks. She was never the same after that.

I wondered if this was the killer's reasoning, his warped sense of right and wrong. He thought himself to be judge and jury it seemed, even though he was the one doing the killing. The "right hand of God" slipped into my mind. His God complex. And then the puzzle pieces started falling together. Her death was personal.

His name was Brad Jenkins. I ran from the situation room to tell Stephanie, taking my notes with me. She was sitting at her desk with a dumbstruck expression.

"Steph. I think I might have a suspect for Stacey Boudreaux's murder." I gave her a summarized version and then handed her my notes. "It all makes sense. Brad Jenkins tried to kill her once before. Her murder was personal. He also knows me, and he would have followed the Medley case once he found out that I was nearly killed. We need to find him."

Stephanie was just staring at me, not saying a word. "Hey, are you all right? Did you hear what I just said?"

She visibly swallowed, and then nodded, taking the notes from my hand. "Yeah, sorry. I was just in a daze, going through these reports."

"Okay, do you want me to get Greg and have him run a check on this guy?"

"No, no, I can do it."

"Hey, what's going on? You don't sound like yourself." I sat on the edge of the desk and looked at her. She had tears in her eyes.

"It's okay, Char. It's just something I have to deal with. I'll be all right. Promise."

Oh. It was then that I remembered how she'd reacted before and thought about the possibility of how we shared a similar attack. I decided not to ask any more questions. I knew how painful it was to talk about.

"All right then. I'm going to head out and check on Nicky. I haven't heard from her today, and I'm getting worried. She should have checked in by now."

"Char.... Oh, okay. See ya later." I stood from her desk and picked up my bag, then waved goodbye on my way out.

I felt so much better knowing we finally had a solid lead. Brad Jenkins. Stacey had had to file a restraining order, and an EPO against him. He'd ended up going to jail for beating her, and not just the one time.

When I got into my vehicle and closed the door, it felt like someone was taking my air. I couldn't breathe. I'd stupidly forgotten to check to make sure no one was in the backseat before I'd opened the door. I had no idea what was going on, and I couldn't see a thing. The copycat killer had found me, and he was going to make me his next victim. Suffocating, I couldn't fight back. The next thing I knew, darkness surrounded me.

Chapter 25

I awoke in a dark room. I couldn't see my hand in front of my face, and my head was freakin' killing me. Had I been knocked out? Where the hell was I? I tried not to panic. Picking myself up from the floor, I blindly felt around the walls for a door. There had to be a door, or a light switch somewhere. I was not going to die today!

Finally, I could feel a small knob, but it wouldn't turn. Dammit! I was locked in from the outside. Screaming, I banged on the door. I continued slamming my fists against the door until I could feel blood trickling down my hands. I would not give up.

I put my ear to the door to see if I could hear anyone, or to at least gauge my surroundings. And then I heard Nicky scream.

"Nicky!!! Noooo! Let me outta here, you bastard! I swear, if you harm a hair on her head, I'll kill you."

"Char? Is that you?" Nicky was crying. I could hear her crying. My heart was breaking. I couldn't help her from inside these damn walls!

"Nicky. I'm locked inside a dark room, and I can't get out. I'll find a way out!"

Then I heard another voice, one I didn't recognize. "Charlotte isn't here, and she won't be helping you, dear Nicky. You're all alone."

"You son of a bitch! I'm right here! Nicky..."

I heard a loud bang coming from somewhere above me, but I couldn't see a damn thing.

"Someone—help me! Please! Get me outta here! Nicky, are you still with me? Can you hear me?"

"Char..." Nicky was sobbing, and the door wouldn't budge.

"Detective Hamilton, you're just in time. Drop your weapon, or Nicky dies."

"Don't you touch her! I'll kill you!" I continued banging against the door and screaming.

I couldn't stop the heaving sobs. I was helpless, and I couldn't do a damn thing to save my best friend, locked up in a damned dark room. And Stephanie! Dear God.

"Stephanie! Save Nicky!" I screamed through the door.

"Lower the knife," Stephanie said to the man, and I could hear her footsteps drawing closer. "You don't want to hurt her."

"Oh, but I do. I am the Harbinger of Death, and she must pay for her sins."

"You sick fuck! Let me outta here! Stephanie, please, help me." I threw myself onto the floor. What was I going to do?

"What sins would that be?" Stephanie asked.

"Drop your weapon, Detective." Then I heard Nicky scream. He must have stabbed or cut her.

I was gonna kill him as soon as I got out of this godforsaken room. I sucked up my tears, stood, and banged on the door—harder this time.

"Answer the question," Stephanie said.

"She has been rendered untrustworthy. She speaks lies and sins against the Almighty. I will render her judgment."

"Nooooo!" And I broke through the door. It shattered into tiny wooden shards, and bright white light blinded me.

When my vision cleared, I looked down. Why was I holding a knife? Why was I in my parents' cellar? And why was Stephanie pointing a gun at me? I looked to the concrete wall, and Nicky was hanging by chains from her wrists.

"Nicky? Stephanie?" I dropped the bloody knife and stood there in shock. "Get her out of those fucking chains!"

I ran to Nicky, crying, pulling on the chains, still not understanding what the hell was going on. My heart was racing, and my mind was in a panic. Something was terribly wrong with me.

"I need the fuckin' keys! I can't loosen the chains. Please help me!" I was crying so much, I could barely breathe. Nicky was hurt, and all I could see was her blood. I needed to help her. She was all I had. My sister. My everything.

"Char, honey," Stephanie said, "step away from Nicky." She was still pointing her gun at me.

"Stop pointing that damn gun at me and help me get her down." I could barely see from the tears pouring down my face. "Please, Stephanie, just help me. I don't know what's going on, but please...she's all I have. Just help me."

Then I fell to the floor in a heap, sobbing uncontrollably. Stephanie dropped her gun to the side and knelt in front of me. "You'll be all right, Char. I'll get her."

I looked up at Nicky, and she was so sad. She had blood running down her left arm. "Nicky... What happened?"

"Oh, honey. I had my suspicions, but I didn't want to believe it. It was always you, Char. I'm so sorry. I still love you, and I'll help you get better." Her hands were free now, and she sat beside me on the floor, holding me, rocking me, while I bawled my eyes out. This couldn't be true. This couldn't be happening. I couldn't have tried to kill my best friend. She was the only person... I just couldn't. No. Not my Nicky. How? I just didn't understand.

"Char, honey, it's time to go," Stephanie said.

"Go where?"

"I have to take you to the station. Greg's upstairs now; he's waiting. I'm so sorry."

"You're not taking her any-fucking-where without me." Nicky stood, picking me up with her. "Is it any wonder her mind broke after everything she's been through? And you tell that Greg, if he has a problem, he can kiss my ass. I'm staying with her."

"Nicky," Stephanie said, "I'm sorry I didn't stop her from leaving the station. I was reading over the reports, putting them together, and I was in shock just trying to process it all." She took a step toward us. "This shouldn't have happened."

"Fuck off, Stephanie. This isn't helping her, and I'm not dead." Nicky squeezed me tighter against her side. "Don't talk about her like she's...like... Just don't."

"All right, I'm so sorry, Nicky." Stephanie turned toward the steps with tears in her eyes. "Char, we won't be making you do a perp walk, or anything like that. All of this will be done hush-hush for now."

I could only nod and hang onto Nicky's waist like my life depended on it. Hell, from what it seemed, my life did depend on it.

Greg had no problem allowing Nicky to ride back to the station with us. He was in tears. I'd never seen him cry. I still had no idea what was going on, or how any of this even happened. I assumed my mind had shattered after the attack, and maybe I did some things I wasn't aware of, but I had no idea how that was even possible, always having people around me at all times. My heart and soul were broken. I didn't know how I would ever come back from this.

Once we arrived at the station, Greg and Stephanie led me to Interview Room Number Two. They didn't handcuff me as promised. I was a wreck. I looked around, not understanding anything, but knowing whatever it was, it was bad. They allowed Nicky to stand just outside the door.

"Char, I hate this, and I'm so sorry." Greg folded his hands together on the table. "I didn't want to believe it, either, but when the forensics came back with your DNA, along with CCTV of you handing a package to some kid next door to your pharmacy, we knew."

I hung my head. "What did I do?"

"I don't think *you* did anything. I'm not a doctor, but based on what I can tell, your personality split, and this is what I can tell ya. Just after you had your staples removed, and Nicky went back to work, your alter personality sought out Stacey, the first victim. He acted as the Harbinger of Death, creating near mirror images of the Medley killings.

"And then the same with Heather. She must have pulled your mother's necklace off during the struggle. We found footage of you retrieving the necklace from the evidence room."

I broke down in tears. "I killed them? I killed Heather and Stacey? But why? Why would I kill my friends? Why?"

Stephanie walked around the table and sat on the edge. "Hon, you didn't know you were doing it. And you probably never will. The only thing I can gather is that your alter personality was trying to take over and get rid of anyone who was ever close to you, or trying to help you in some way."

"But why Jessica? What did she ever do to me? I don't understand any of this. I carved threats into my own walls?" I threw my head onto the table and wept. None of this made any sense. I couldn't have killed these people. This had to be some kind of mind game. Why would they do this to me?

"And the package," Greg said. "I'm so sorry. The DNA report came back as Georgia Henderson."

I looked up in shock. "What? How? I've only been to her office twice! Once for a session, and once to pick up a prescription. How is that even possible?"

"Her receptionist had left due to a family emergency after you called. Georgia gave you the prescription, and it's all on video. We saw you do it." Stephanie leaned in. "Char, we'll get you the medical help you need. You will get better. I..."

And she started crying. I couldn't take anymore. I rocked back and forth in my chair. I had killed people, alter personality or not, I had done it.

Three Weeks Later

I was sitting inside my cell located in Louisiana State Penitentiary. I was supposed to be on the mental ward, but it seemed there was no such place. Everyone was thrown together. But because I was a cop, I wasn't placed in general population, and I guessed that was one small favor. I was going to die in this place anyway; there was no need in rushing it along.

I attended daily sessions with psychiatrists; one had diagnosed me with dissociative personality disorder and then attempted to explain to me what had happened, and how my mind had literally split in half. Apparently, I hadn't been able to cope with the attack, and losing my parents, so an alter had appeared, taking over. I still couldn't wrap my mind around it. She'd said it was possible that this had stemmed from seeing my birthparents murdered when I was seven.

I barely had any emotions left after taking the medications they'd prescribed. It was for the best, I assumed. I didn't *want* to feel after what I'd done, and I deserved to be where I was—rotting away in a cell.

Rocking in my lone possession, a white rocking chair Nicky had insisted they allow me to have, I gazed outside my small, barred window. It was cloudy, just like my mood. I wrapped my arms around myself and thought of better times: back when I was free, back when my parents were alive, and when I could see Nicky's smiling face every day.

I'd signed everything over to Nicky once I was put away. She deserved it, and I wanted her to be happy. The one person in this world who truly loved me, and I loved her. I missed her terribly.

A lone tear escaped my eye, and then I heard a voice. "Little birdie, little birdie—you can be free. Let's kill them all—just you and me."

I turned in my chair, looking to see where the voice was coming from. My cell door was locked, and I was all alone. No one was in here but me.

I slammed my hands over my ears and rocked in my chair. "Never again." I repeated, "Never again."

The End

To read more of Angela Sanders' books, you can find them on her website https://angelasandersbooks.com

For information on Angela's latest book releases and book news, sign up for her newsletter here:

https://landing.mailerlite.com/webforms/landing/f6r4o9

Made in the USA
Middletown, DE
05 June 2019